MISTRESS OF ALL EVIL
A TALE OF THE DARK FAIRY

MISTRESS OF ALL EVIL

A TALE OF THE DARK FAIRY

BY SERENA VALENTINO

DISNEP PRESS

LOS ANGELES • NEW YORK

In memory of my little sister Jesse.
My own beautiful dark fairy.
—Serena Valentino

MISTRESS OF ALL EVIL

A TALE OF THE DARK FAIRY

The Dark Fairy's castle was eerily silhouetted against a tempestuous sky by a magnificent spiral of glowing green mist. Suddenly, a brilliant burst of green light shot up from the highest tower, warning every nearby creature that Maleficent was in a terrible rage. Her goons shuddered as the castle shook violently with the power of her anger, sending her beloved murder of crows into flight. For nearly sixteen years, her creatures had been searching for the princess Aurora. But it had all been in vain. Now the girl was home in King Stefan's castle for her sixteenth birthday, ready to take her place at the royal court.

Maleficent paced back and forth in her private chamber. She hadn't been able to reach the odd sisters by raven or crow. "Why didn't they listen to me?" she muttered furiously. "They should *never* have trusted Ursula!"

Maleficent needed the sisters now more than ever, and she feared they were lost to her. She went to the enchanted mirror hanging on her wall. The three sisters had given it to her many years before.

"Show me Lucinda! Show me Ruby! Show me Martha!" she commanded. The mirror's surface swirled with a glowing violet light. The Dark Fairy had never quite mastered mirror magic like the odd sisters, and she seldom used their gift. Nevertheless, after a moment, hazy images of the sisters appeared in the glass. They were wandering aimlessly through a large mirrored chamber. They seemed to be calling out a name over and over again, but Maleficent couldn't discern their words.

"Lucinda! Can you hear me? Sisters! I need you!" Maleficent cried. For a moment, she thought that the sisters had heard her, because they abruptly stopped their ceaseless wandering.

"Sisters! Where are you? I need your help with Aurora!" Maleficent shouted.

Suddenly, Lucinda grew more distinct in the mirror. Her face flickered in the swirling purple haze of magic as she ushered frantic orders to the Dark Fairy. "You must get into that castle, Maleficent! Go by fire! Go by smoke! Go by rhyme! Go by any means available to you, but go! Create the mundane instrument of her doom if you must and send her to the land of dreams. We will be waiting for her. But you must find a way to make sure she never wakes! Our powers are not the same in this place. It's all up to you! Now go!"

And then, as quickly as she had appeared, Lucinda was gone. Maleficent only saw her own green face reflected in the mirror's surface. No matter how many times Maleficent called for Lucinda and her sisters, she couldn't summon them again. She smashed the mirror into tiny pieces with her staff, angrier than ever with the odd sisters for their foolishness.

Maleficent turned to her beloved pet raven Diablo, who was perched on her shoulder. "It seems the odd sisters are lost in the land of dreams. I told them something like this would happen if they helped Ursula! They didn't listen, the *fools*!"

Maleficent tightened her grip on her staff. The green sphere on the end began to glow. "I will use fire, smoke, and rhyme! Those meddlesome fairies thought they could keep their darling Rose hidden from me. They thought they could keep her safe. But I know the king and queen have their precious princess within their castle at this very moment!"

Maleficent stormed to her fireplace. "I shall use fire!" she cried as she slammed her staff soundly on the stone floor. Her castle rumbled as a large blaze appeared in her fireplace, followed by a matching fire in Princess Aurora's chamber. Through the flames, Maleficent could see Aurora crying. "Poor dear, she doesn't know she's betrothed to her one true love! All the better.

"Now I shall use rhyme," Maleficent declared, extinguishing the fire and closing her eyes as the words of her dark spell swirled through her thoughts.

Bring me to their cherished Rose
And bring this chapter to a close.
By smoke, by fire, and by night,
Touch the spindle I shall ignite.
Sleep will come to their fair Rose,
Forever trapped in her repose.

A tiny wisp of smoke curled ominously from Aurora's fireplace. Maleficent's yellow eyes contrasted brilliantly with the fireplace's darkness as she transported herself to King Stefan's castle.

Enchant the Rose with burning light,
No fear, no sorrow, no flight from fright.
Let her follow without despair
So she may slumber forever without care.

An odious green orb appeared in the princess's room, casting an unearthly green glow on the girl's

pale face as she rose from her vanity. The luminescent sphere danced before her eyes, bewitching
her to follow it through an enchanted passageway
Maleficent had conjured in the fireplace. The spellbound princess followed the orb up a cold, dark
stairway with an archway that eerily resembled a
tombstone. Maleficent heard the troublesome good
fairies calling their Rose's name. With a flick of
her hand, she closed off the passageway, leaving the
good fairies behind.

Higher and higher Aurora climbed, until she
reached the tallest tower in the castle. The Dark
Fairy transformed the malignant glowing ball into
a spinning wheel. At last her curse would be
complete.

As the wheel spins, so does time,
Unstoppable and divine.
Weaving my spell of endless sleep,
In dreamscape she shall keep.

The princess reached for the spindle but

hesitated. A force within her seemed to be struggling against Maleficent's evil spell.

"Touch the spindle! Touch it, I say!" Maleficent commanded. Her dark magic prevailed over the poor princess, who reached out and lightly touched the spindle's point. The sharp needle pierced her skin, sending a sickening feeling through her entire body. She felt all the life draining from her as her world went black. The princess fell to the floor at Maleficent's feet, hidden beneath the Dark Fairy's long robes.

At that moment, the three good fairies burst into the room, their little faces filled with fear and worry.

Maleficent smirked at the trio. "You poor simple *fools*! Thinking you could defeat me! *Me!* The mistress of *all* evil!"

Finally, she had the princess Aurora.

After all those years, her curse had put their beloved princess to sleep, just as she'd decreed. Their attempts to keep her safe had failed. With a flourish, Maleficent swept her cloak to one side.

"Well, here's your precious princess!" she added, cackling triumphantly.

The three good fairies gasped at the ghastly scene. Their beautiful Rose's lifeless body lay on the cold stone floor. Her tiara lay beside her, like an omen that she would never become queen.

CHAPTER I

THE DARK FAIRY

Black crows circled overhead, following the Dark Fairy as she made her way through the tangled forest. With each step she took, the trees grew increasingly dense. The forest was a living thing, moving and breathing. Its vines curled themselves around everything in her path, unknowingly creating a deep, penetrating darkness as they ensnared the treetops and obscured the sky. In the shadows, the Dark Fairy could keep the grasping trees and vines at bay. Even though she didn't understand that aspect of her magic, Maleficent used it to her advantage. Contrary to the tales surrounding the Dark Fairy, the vines weren't entirely subject to her will. She had heard stories about how she could control nature. How she could direct terrible forests to destroy her enemies. It was ironic, given the truth. Nature had cursed her for a past transgression. Nature was her enemy, and this forest was no different.

Though Maleficent could keep the forest in check in the shadows, she wasn't entirely sure what would happen once she left the protection of the darkness provided by the canopy. She wondered if she would be able to fight off the forest when she wandered into the full blaze of the sun.

For now, it gave her great satisfaction to see the emerald greenery wither and retreat before her as heat emanated from her staff. The trees on nearby cliffs were joining with the vines. The foliage banded together, creating an army of sorts against her.

There is nothing more frightening to a forest than the threat of fire.

The Dark Fairy laughed as she sent a surge of green light toward the branches, which recoiled from the heat. She wished the forest would give her a reason to set it ablaze. But she reined in her desire for destruction, reminding herself of her purpose and destination.

Maleficent resented having to travel at that time; she hated being so far away from the Sleeping Beauty and the lovestruck prince who threatened her plans. A few short days earlier, the princess had pricked her finger on a spindle, just as Maleficent's curse had decreed. Maleficent had ordered her goons to abduct Prince Phillip and bring him back to her dungeons, where he would be well away from the sleeping princess. She couldn't have him intervening in her masterful plan. But even so, the Dark Fairy needed help. She needed witches—powerful witches who could help her bind Sleeping Beauty's curse so that the princess would never wake. If she couldn't kill the princess, Maleficent would have to content herself with Aurora's forever dwelling in the land of dreams. So the Dark Fairy ventured to Morningstar Kingdom.

How she wished she was traveling by her preferred method of flames. But she wanted the witches at Morningstar Castle to know she was approaching. She wanted to give them time to grieve the loss of the sea witch and the odd sisters before she arrived. Maleficent knew the reason for her visit would be obscured by fear if she showed up without warning. So she took her time and walked slowly to Morningstar Kingdom, following her beloved crows. The canopy was so thick now that she could not see her birds flying overhead, but her magic was strong and it allowed her to see the path that lay before them through their eyes. She loved that aspect of her magic more than any other. It made her feel like she was flying with them, untethered from the world. But Maleficent did not need magic to find her way. The witches' hearts drew her to them, shining like a brilliant beacon among the ruins of some of the greatest witches of their age.

Maleficent had sent Diablo ahead to Morningstar Kingdom. As he circled the castle, she could see the extent of the carnage and destruction left in Ursula's wake. Engulfed in the remains of the sea witch, the ancient fortress was almost pulsing with hate. Maleficent had no love for Ursula and didn't grieve her loss. In fact, she thought the many kingdoms on land and sea were better off without such a power-hungry and foolish witch. Ursula had put all their lives in peril by creating a spell so dangerous that the odd sisters were now suffering its consequences.

Maleficent couldn't see into the future like some witches and fairies, but she was a good judge of character. She had sensed the amount of power Ursula had been hoarding, and she had been certain the sea witch would betray the sisters. She only wished that the odd sisters had listened to her warning. Maleficent had once loved the odd sisters deeply, though lately they were more like strange relatives she barely tolerated, and avoided at every opportunity. She struggled to remember them as they once had been, to remember how she'd loved them. But that feeling—*love*—was a mere memory.

Perhaps that was for the best. The odd sisters had become troublesome nuisances, growing more and more deranged as the years had passed. She could no longer feel their presence in the world—or in her heart—and she suddenly felt a kinship with the sisters that she hadn't felt for some time. She tried to remember what it was like to care for them—or for anyone, for that matter. But she couldn't. And now the sisters were lost to her; too far gone for her magic to reach them. It almost made her sad.

Sadness. That feeling had eluded her for so long that her memory of it was like a faded dream. And that was where those sisters were: in a dream, lost forever to the waking world.

Wandering in dream. Alone.

Maleficent didn't want to think of what the sisters dreamed or what their dream world was like. Living in the dreamscape meant inhabiting the darkest and deepest places of the mind. She couldn't fathom what secrets sprang to life for the sisters in their new reality. She shuddered at the thought of the land of dreams being invaded by the sisters' nightmares, and she wondered if they would find the sleeping Rose in her own corner of the dream- scape.

Damn those sisters to Hades, with their mirrors, rhymes, and lunacy! They just had *to save their precious little sister!*

But the old queen in the mirror had said it best. *"Like many of us, Maleficent, those loathsome sisters were unable to think clearly when their family was in peril."*

Maleficent had laughed at the old queen, whom she knew as Grimhilde. For her to be speaking to Maleficent of concern for *family* of all things . . . But she'd choked down her words like jagged stones, unwilling to speak with the old queen about her daughter, Snow White, who now thrived as queen of her own kingdom.

The thought made Maleficent sick.

What must it be like to live such a charmed life? To live untouched by the strife that had been ripping so many kingdoms apart? But that was the old queen's doing, wasn't it? Somehow her magic was even greater now than it had been when she was alive. Grimhilde reached beyond the veil of death to keep her daughter and her family safe. Perhaps that was Grimhilde's punishment for trying to kill

Snow White when she was a child. Grimhilde had taken her own father's place in the magic mirror. She would forever be Snow White's slave, as Grimhilde's father had once been hers. She was cursed to be Snow White's protector—never at rest. She was always watching Snow White while she slept, forever shielding Snow's children and grandchildren. Eternally bringing happiness to that infernal brat and her brood.

Grimhilde's love for her daughter sat in Maleficent's stomach like a cold stone. It caused a tingling sensation that told Maleficent this was something she should feel. An inkling that this was something that would have touched her heart. But she pushed that inkling down with the others that lived in the pit of her stomach. She imagined they all looked like broken pieces of headstone. She wondered how they all fit together there and how it was possible for someone so small to carry so much. Sometimes she felt the weight of them would crush her, yet it never did. She supposed everyone carried their burdens there. It seemed like the perfect place—close to the heart, but not dangerously so.

The odd sisters had once told her that Grimhilde had also kept her pain in her stomach. To the old queen, it had been like jagged glass slicing at her insides. Maleficent wondered what was worse: the heaviness of her burden or the pain of Grimhilde's. The odd sisters would have said both were capable of destroying their hosts. But Maleficent felt like the weight of her sorrow grounded her and kept her steady. Without her pain, she might just float away.

The odd sisters had decreed that the brat queen and her family were to be left alone, so as not to anger Grimhilde. But Snow White wasn't entirely untouched by the odd sisters, was she? The old queen Grimhilde could not control her daughter's dreams. That was not her providence. That was not her domain.

Dreams belonged to the good fairies and to the sisters three.

CHAPTER II

REQUIEM

Two witches, divergent in age and in schools of magic, though with very similar hearts and sensibilities, stood on the windy cliffs near Morningstar Castle. The sea bubbled with putrid black foam, and the sky was filled with a thick, deep purple smoke that obscured the daylight and enshrouded Morningstar Kingdom in a veil of darkness.

Everywhere Circe looked, she saw manifestations of Ursula that had exploded onto their surroundings. It was sickening to behold. The destruction blackened the shores and saddened the witches' hearts. Circe would have to use her magic to bring life and growth back to the kingdom, but she couldn't bring herself to face the task—not just yet. She knew that in doing so, she would be obliterating what remained of her old friend Ursula.

"An old friend who ripped your soul from your body, turning it into a husk. Yours and countless other souls," Nanny reminded her, reading her thoughts.

Circe just smiled weakly, knowing Nanny was right. But she saw *that* Ursula, the one who had betrayed her, as someone quite different from the one she had known as a girl. Ursula had been a wild and charismatic character. She had been Circe's sisters' dearest friend and like an aunt to Circe—a great witch who had brought Circe bobbles and had told her stories of the sea. This creature, the *thing* she'd become, wasn't the Ursula Circe loved. Ursula had become someone else, someone consumed by grief, anger, and the desire for power. A woman who had been driven to the depths of despair by a brother who loathed her. Circe remembered going to Ursula that day; she remembered thinking someone else—no, *something* else—was looking at her from behind Ursula's eyes. It was chilling to remember.

Circe had felt like running from her that day, but she had told herself it was all her imagination. She'd reminded herself that she'd always trusted Ursula. She had never imagined Ursula would harm her. But if Circe was really honest with herself, there was no way she could have denied that the *creature* inhabiting her old friend that day had meant to hurt her. Circe just hadn't wanted to see it then. She had denied her fear, pushed it aside, and willed herself to see the woman she loved. And that was how she had allowed herself to be captured by the dreaded sea witch. How Ursula had been able to use her as a pawn to manipulate her sisters.

The woman she loved had betrayed her.

No, Ursula betrayed herself. And now she was dead, rendered to nothing more than smoke, sludge, and ash. She was beyond Circe's help now. Still, Circe tortured herself with questions. Why hadn't Ursula come to her in honesty? Why hadn't she told Circe the whole story—the story she had told Circe's sisters? Circe would have helped Ursula destroy Triton without the need to involve his youngest daughter. None of it made any sense. Ursula must have known that Circe had the power to destroy Triton, but she also knew Circe would never endanger the life of Ariel.

Damn Triton for the damage he did to his sister! Damn him to Hades for his complicity! Damn him for making Ursula hide who she truly was. Damn him for turning her into a loathsome creature by his own design!

It was taking everything she had not to cast curses at King Triton. She wanted to tell him that when she'd touched Ursula's necklace, she'd seen everything Ursula had ever experienced—the causes of all her rage, sorrow, and pain. Circe had heard every foul word and witnessed every hateful deed Ursula had endured from Triton. It had ripped at Circe's heart, as it surely must have done to Ursula's. Maybe one day Circe would throw Triton's words back at him. But she wouldn't do it now. Not while her hate for him was still strong in her heart. The pain was too fresh.

And then something quite sad occurred to Circe:

family was capable of causing more harm than anyone. Family was true heartbreak. They could rip out your heart like no one else. They could destroy your spirit and leave you alone in the tangled depths of despair. Family could ruin you, more than a lover might, and surely more than even the dearest of friends could. Family could hold its power over you.

Circe knew all too well what it was like to have her heart broken by family. She had her own troublesome sisters—the odd sisters. They could scream a house down with their rage and tantrums. But her sisters loved her ferociously—far too well. She never worried on that account. She knew she had their love and always would no matter what befell them. Now her sisters were trapped in a sleeping death, all because she'd left them and had allowed herself to be tricked by the sea witch. All because she had been angry with them for loving her too much. They loved her so much that they would've destroyed anyone or done anything to protect her. And how had she repaid them?

She'd condemned them for haunting the Beast.

She'd screamed at them for putting Tulip's life in danger. They'd been responsible for many deaths and many transgressions. Circe was sure she didn't even know about all of them. But none of those things seemed to matter now. Not while her sisters lay broken, as if dead, under the glass dome of the Morningstar solarium. Their eyes were wide open. As hard as Circe had tried, she could not close them. Did her sisters know what had happened to them? Did they remember battling Ursula's spell to save their little sister? Did they remember fighting their own spell, so embedded with hatred that it took all their strength to break? They looked haunted to Circe as they stared into nothingness. No magic would give her sisters the appearance of peacefulness. It seemed even in their sleep they were being punished, paying for every act of wickedness they had ever committed and for their part in Ursula's demise. Circe wondered if her sisters could see what remained of Ursula staining the glass dome and billowing overhead, thick, black, and putrid. Did they feel Ursula's hate emanating from every surface of the kingdom? Was Circe prolonging her sisters' torture by not cleansing Morningstar? It was time to move on—to rid the castle of Ursula's remains. But how? Where would Circe's magic send them? What was the protocol when a witch of Ursula's caliber died? What were the words? Circe's head spun with the questions.

How do you honor a witch who betrayed you?

"We put her to rest," Nanny said gently, wrapping her arm around Circe's shoulders. "And we cleanse the land. Come, my sweet one, I will help you."

CHAPTER III

THE GREAT
SEA QUEEN

The Lighthouse of the Gods shone magnificently in the brilliant sunlight as the witches stood silently in honor of the sea witch. Pink, purple, and golden blossoms showered down on the crowd assembled to mourn the passing of a great and terrible queen. Nanny had put Ursula's remains in a ship constructed of delicate golden straw, adorned with beautiful sea-shells and glittering white sand. The ship sparkled in the sunlight and was reflected beautifully by the rippling water. The waves glittered with the golden straw that was mingling with the blossoms in the water. Circe nudged the ship gently, sending Ursula farther into the waves. "Good-bye, great one," she said softly.

Ursula looked peaceful, and Circe was thankful to Nanny for bringing Ursula's remains together so they could honor her. It was a proper tribute that befitted the queen of the sea. Circe knew if Triton had given Ursula her rightful place by his side as ruler, she would still be alive. And that was what hurt Circe's heart most.

Circe held Nanny's hand tightly as they said good-bye. It tugged at Circe's heart to let her friend go, but she was thankful she had Nanny, Princess Tulip, and Prince Popinjay by her side. They all looked pensive as they took in the magnitude of the great loss. And it was unnoticed by anyone else, but Circe saw Popinjay had taken Tulip's little hand in his. He squeezed it gently, as if to remind Tulip that he was there for her if she needed him. Circe smiled, because she knew the beautiful princess could meet any challenge that came her way without Popinjay's help. Nevertheless, Circe was happy he was there for Tulip.

Triton was not in attendance. He had been warned that he was not welcome, so Circe was surprised to see that merfolk from Triton's kingdom had come to pay their respects. She had to wonder if Triton had declared his complicity to his people and if that was why some of them seemed to be truly mourning Ursula's passing. Did some of them have pity for Ursula—or at least understand her motives after they'd heard her story? Perhaps they were simply there to see with their own eyes that the sea witch was no longer a threat. Circe didn't know.

One of the mermaids from Triton's court swam up to Circe and Nanny. She was pretty, with a small pointed crown made of delicate coral. Her voice had a familiar soft ring to it.

"Hello, my name is Attina," the young mermaid said. "I'm Triton's eldest daughter. He sent me here to see that his sister was given a proper funeral." She looked at the witches, who were staring blankly back at her. Out of nervousness, she kept talking. "I hope you don't mind my sisters and I being here."

Nanny looked at the group of mermaids. All

of them were looking in their direction, worried expressions on their faces. "If you are here to honor her, dear, then you are more than welcome."

Circe looked at Attina suspiciously. "I'm surprised you're here after everything Ursula did to your little sister."

Attina smiled, but her eyes were sad. "And I'm surprised you honor her so graciously after she nearly destroyed you." Circe could sense the young woman was conflicted. The mermaid was torn between her loyalty to her little sister Ariel and her obligation to the woman she hadn't known was her aunt. "I'm here for my father. And for Ursula, for the woman she could have been had my father not ruined all that was good within her," Attina added.

Her answer was good enough for Circe. "You are welcome here, then, Attina. Tell your father we gave Ursula a funeral fit for a queen. That's who she was and who she shall always be—queen of the sea."

The mermaid swam back to her sisters. Together, they watched a procession of ships escort Ursula's exquisitely constructed ship of golden straw farther out to sea. Fireworks shot from the ships, casting golden lights into the sky. Beneath them, Ursula's ship was taken by the tides, the fine straw dispersing, and releasing her remains to the sea, where she would rest forever in tranquility. Circe took a deep breath and exhaled slowly. Her old friend was finally at peace.

For a moment, Circe felt at ease. She was experiencing one of those perfect moments in time when everything was beautiful, even the heartbreak. And she wished that she could live in that moment just a little bit longer. But the present was quickly becoming the past as she heard Nanny gasp next to her. In the distance, the witches saw a large mass. It looked like a living forest entangled by thorny vines, climbing and twisting its way toward the rocky cliffs beyond Morningstar Castle. And with it came a terrible looming darkness that harbored something sinister. Soaring above the darkness, through the turbulent clouds streaked with swirls of green light, were Maleficent's crows—the very portents of evil.

Circe could feel the fearsome forest's energy with her magic; she knew the forest was not coming to destroy them. It was trying to protect Morningstar from the Dark Fairy.

CHAPTER IV

The Land of Dreams

In the land of dreams, things worked differently than they did practically anywhere else. Almost anything was possible in the dreamscape. The land was frozen in a perpetual twilight. The never-setting sun cast an ethereal glow and created a special brand of magic known to some as the golden hour. All inhabitants of the land of dreams occupied their own spaces, like many little hamlets in a kingdom of an unfathomable size. Each chamber was composed almost entirely of mirrors. And if the dreamers could master the magic of the mirrors, they would get a glimpse of the outside world. However, the dreamscape's magic remained elusive to most of the realm's visitors and befuddled some of its more long-term occupants, making it a terribly lonely place.

Magic was not something unfamiliar to Aurora. Although her fairy caretakers had hidden their powers from her for the past sixteen years, she had always sensed something magical about them. Aurora never talked about it with her fairy aunts, but she knew when magic was near. She didn't know why, but it hadn't frightened her. She could also sense magic moving in other kingdoms, even in those farthest from hers. So it wasn't difficult for her to puzzle out how to use the magic in the land of dreams. Aurora reasoned the magic one could wield in that world wasn't particularly powerful. If it were, she would have found a way to wake herself. It seemed Maleficent's sleeping curse was too powerful for the dreamscape's magic to overcome—besides, the magic in that place wasn't direct or even particularly practical. It was rather basic and mundane, yet somehow simultaneously unpredictable and chaotic. Nevertheless, the princess had harnessed it to see into the outside world.

Aurora's corner of the dreamscape was an octagon chamber built entirely of towering rectangular mirrors. She could see reflected in the glass a myriad of past and present events throughout the many kingdoms. Initially, she had wondered if the room and images were merely a dream, but she had decided that they were real. That simple decision gave her the power to control the images that appeared in the mirror. Aurora had quickly realized all she had to do was think about someone she wanted to see and their image would appear in one of the mirrored glass panels. She could see where that person was and what they were doing, which made her feel less lonely in the strange realm. That brought her comfort, even if she knew she might never again walk in the waking world.

It was strange having so much knowledge at once and having so little power to direct her own fate. But she listened, she watched, and she learned. Aurora discovered that her betrothed was actually the young man she had fallen in love with in the forest. She learned that Maleficent had arranged to keep him captive in her dungeon. She knew her fairy aunts had changed her name to Rose to protect her, and she knew why. She knew everything. She even thought she knew why Maleficent was doing all this, but that part was too terrifying to think about. So she focused on other people. Aurora looked in on her fairy aunts, who seemed to be planning a visit to witches Aurora didn't know. Sometimes Aurora looked in on her mother and father while they slept. She tried to see what they dreamed, but she couldn't. The princess supposed their dreams were their own. She even tried to find them in her dream world, but it seemed that traveling between the chambers was impossible. So Aurora tried to be content with acquainting herself with her own story. She watched events from her past scroll by in the many mirrors of her chamber. Flashing images cascaded across her vision and she saw herself as a baby on the day of her christening. There, in the dreamscape, Aurora first laid eyes on Maleficent, the tall stoic Dark Fairy. She was probably the most beautiful creature Aurora had ever seen, standing there among all her parents' guests. Aurora had witnessed how she'd become trapped in this realm, trapped in a sleeping death. Why she'd spent so many years with her fairy caretakers, believing that she was someone else: a girl called Rose who never thought she was a princess. She honestly didn't know what was worse: living her life in the dream world, or living in a world where everyone lied to her.

A voice echoed through her chamber: "Oh, we know. We know which is worse."

Aurora spun in circles, searching all the mirrors. She couldn't see who was talking to her.

"Over here, Princess. Or should we call you *Rose?*"

Aurora whirled around again. Peeking out on the right side of one of the mirrors was a strange-looking woman. She was wearing a bright red voluminous dress cinched very tightly at the waist. Her tiny pointed boots stuck out from under the hem of her skirt. Aurora wasn't sure why, but there was something sinister about those boots. They looked like two slinking creatures slithering out from under a curtain of blood. Aurora reminded herself that this was the dream world and she shouldn't let her imagination run wild. But nothing about the woman seemed right. Her features were all out of proportion: her deathly pale skin, large bulbous eyes, pitch-black hair, and tiny red lips. Nothing quite fit. Just then, two more women who looked exactly the same entered the mirrors on either side of the first, creating a trio.

"Yes, we are three!" they sang together as one.

"This has to be a dream," Aurora said to herself. "These women can't be real."

"Oh, we're real, Princess," the first woman said.

"Welcome to the land of dreams, little one," the second one chimed in.

"Yes, we have been searching for you," the third one added.

"Maleficent will be happy we found you," all three said in unison. At that, the sister witches began to cackle, their laughter sending chills through Aurora's heart.

CHAPTER V

SHE BELONGS
TO THE CROWS

As Nanny and Circe watched Maleficent draw nearer to Morningstar Kingdom, Nanny's thoughts drifted to places long forgotten. The distant places she'd previously preferred to keep locked away in the deep recesses of her mind. But something inexplicable was happening. The closer the Dark Fairy got to Morningstar Castle, the more Nanny began to remember. It was a painful process, because the memories weren't just her own; they were Maleficent's, as well. And in that moment, Nanny resented having the ability to read minds and to feel her loved ones' emotions. She almost wished for the days when she thought she was just Tulip's nanny, unaware of her powers or her past, or the great love she had for Maleficent. But rather than fighting the memories, she succumbed to them. She let them wash over her like a torrent of half-remembered dreams. And she opened her mind to Circe, sharing her thoughts.

Maleficent had been born in the Fairylands, in the hollow of a tree filled with screeching crows. She was little and defenseless, and she seemed to be made up entirely of sharp edges. Her features were pointy and her skin had a milky-green pallor. Terrible nubby horns were starting to emerge from her bony little head. Nothing about her was right. Nothing at all.

All the fairies feared her, because they found her appearance disturbing. They'd left her there in that tree, alone, for no one knew who had abandoned her there. If her parents hadn't wanted her, then surely the fairies didn't, either. For all they knew, she was actually an ogre. Or something too vile for even the likes of ogres. Besides, she didn't have wings or pleasant features. And there was a distinct air of evil about her, so clearly she *couldn't* be a fairy. No, she wasn't a fairy at all. At least, that was what the fairies told themselves, to console themselves when they stayed up late at night, wondering if they'd done the right thing by leaving the defenseless little creature in the hollow of an old tree.

Whatever her origins, she belonged to the crows. *The crows will care for her,* the fairies told themselves. *She must have been born of their magic.*

After all, everyone knew crows were evil.

The fairies called her Maleficent. They had named her after Saturn, because of its unfavorable influence, and after Mars, a malicious god known to cause destruction and war. For that was what the fairies saw in her future: malice, devastation, and conflict.

So the crows cared for her. They brought her food from the tables of other fairies. Sometimes they even took clothes off drying lines so that she would have something to wear. The clothes smelled of sunshine and flowers. They were warm from the sun and soft on her small frame.

And so it went until Nanny, the One of Legends came home to the Fairylands. She had come to take her place once again as headmistress of the Fairy Academy.

It was twilight when the One of Legends arrived in the Fairylands. Her light blue eyes sparkled and her silver hair fell to her shoulders in loose curls. The sunset was a deep purple, with brilliant wisps of pink and orange streaking the sky. Already the stars were visible, and they seemed to twinkle more brightly when the One of Legends was near.

The One of Legends smiled, happy to be home again. But her smile faltered as she spied the young fairy crouched in the hollow tree. Maleficent was four by that time and still all sharp edges. She was nothing like the round little fairies that flitted around the Fairylands like fluffy bumblebees pollinating the flowers with glittering magic. To the other fairies, Maleficent looked ill. She was too skinny, too green, and far too pinched-faced. And her horns—those *horrible* horns—made her look more evil than anything else. But the One of

Legends saw something others didn't see. She saw a lost little girl who needed love.

"What are you doing in this tree, child? Where are your parents?" the One of Legends asked.

The little girl didn't answer. She wasn't used to speaking to anyone other than her crows. In fact, she was almost certain that this was the first time someone had ever spoken directly to her. Though the woman's face was kind, Maleficent wasn't used to anyone making eye contact with her. She certainly didn't expect to see a pleasant expression when someone looked upon her. Usually, the fairies wrinkled their noses at her—when they bothered to look at her at all.

"Speak, child! Who are you?" Nanny inquired.

Maleficent tried to speak, but she couldn't. The only sound that came from her lips was a terrible screech that reminded Nanny of a hoarse crow.

My goodness, this poor girl has never used her voice. Not once. Not even to cry. The realization broke Nanny's heart.

Maleficent wasn't sure if she even had a voice.

Her crows spoke to her in their own way, and they understood her without her having to talk.

The One of Legends understood the problem. With a wave of her hand, she gave the small green fairy the courage to find her voice.

"Now speak, dear," she said encouragingly.

"Hell . . . o."

Maleficent's voice sounded like the croak of a frog, scratchy and strained. But she had spoken for the first time! It was frightening and exciting at once.

"Well, that's a start, isn't it, my dear? And what's your name?"

"They . . . they call me . . . Maleficent."

"Who, dear, the crows? Who calls you Maleficent?"

Maleficent shook her head slowly. "The fairies."

"Do they, now?" Nanny knew *exactly* why her sister and the other fairies had named the child Maleficent. It sent a hot surge of anger coursing through her body. Nanny tried not to let it register on her face as she smiled down at the little girl.

"And why, may I ask, are you here all alone?"

Nanny continued. "Where are your parents? I will have quite a thing or two to say to them for leaving such a little fairy alone in the cold with no one but crows for company!"

"This is where I live. The crows *are* my parents."

When the One of Legends looked up at the crows, she saw concern in their eyes and she knew that the girl was telling the truth. *How in the Fairylands could my sister have stood by and let this happen? Abandoning the girl like this? Leaving her to be cared for by the* crows? *It's a disgrace.*

"Will you let me take you home with me, little one?" Nanny asked. "I can care for you."

Slowly, Maleficent shook her head. "No."

"No? Why not, may I ask?" Nanny tried not to laugh. Maleficent looked so stern, and so decisive, especially for one so young.

"I don't want to leave my crows!"

"Then we shall bring them with us! How does that sound?"

And looking up at her crows for a moment, Maleficent slowly nodded.

Maleficent's life utterly changed that evening. Nanny could see that no one had ever treated Maleficent like she was anything other than something to be feared. She was glad to be able to give Maleficent the love she deserved. Maleficent felt safe with her and called her Nanny. And that was what she was—her nanny—though Nanny cared for Maleficent like she was her own child. Together they lived in a beautiful Tudor-style cottage with gingerbread trimmings and large-paned windows. Nanny magically replanted Maleficent's crow tree in the front garden, and she fashioned a wonderful tree house just for Maleficent so that she could visit her crows whenever she wished. Nanny insisted on always keeping a window open so that the crows could come into the cottage whenever they liked. They often flitted in and out, checking on their little fairy to be sure Nanny was treating her well, which she always was. She loved Maleficent dearly and was unspeakably happy to give the special girl a home and family to call her own.

CHAPTER VI

THE WITCH'S DAUGHTER

Queen Snow White woke in terror. It was the same old nightmare: she was running through a tangled forest with grasping trees scratching her as she fought to escape their clutches. She almost expected to be covered in cuts but found herself unharmed.

"Momma?" Snow looked for her mother's reflection in the mirror on her bedside table. "Are you there?"

But the old queen didn't answer.

Snow looked around her room at the other reflective surfaces. She found nothing other than her own pale face. It was a strange feeling, waking up without her mother smiling back at her from one of the mirrors. Snow glanced around her room at her things, trying to shake off the terrible feeling of her dream. Everything was in its place. There was nothing strange or amiss as there normally would be when she thought she'd awoken from a nightmare but was actually still dreaming. This was her room, with its deep red tapestries, adorned with golden trees and tiny blackbirds, hanging on the walls. This was her bed, with its light petal-pink curtains draped around the four cherry-oak pillars. She looked around her room again at the many mirrors held in beautiful antique gold frames of various sizes. Yes, everything was as it should be. She was safe. That was what her mother always said to her when she woke up startled, wasn't it? *Look! You're in your own room. You're safe, my bird.* But the shadows of this nightmare remained. She could still feel the looming danger of something pursuing her as she searched the dark corners of her room, hoping she wasn't still dreaming.

I need to speak with my mother.

Snow had to tell her about the other part of her

dream. It was a new nightmare—one that reminded her of a story her mother had told her when she was very small.

The story of the Dragon Witch who put a young girl to sleep.

Why do witches always put young girls to sleep in these stories?

Snow White's own story was very similar. Her mother had put her to sleep. But that was many years past, so long ago that Snow rarely thought of it. The Dragon Witch had been plaguing Snow's dreams for many nights. That much she knew. But the actual events of the bad dream always escaped her upon her waking. All she remembered was the forest from her childhood. She'd been trying to capture her memory of the Dragon Witch dream so she could share it her mother, but it was like a forgotten word or name she couldn't grasp. Snow knew this dream was important. She knew this nightmare held meaning. And now that she finally remembered it, her mother wasn't there.

Where is she?

Snow White dressed quickly in one of her favorite gowns. It was a red velvet dress decorated with embroidered silver birds and shiny black beads that sparkled in the light. She sat at her vanity, looking at her mirror as she brushed her thick black hair, brilliantly streaked with silver at each of her temples. She watched the curls bounce back with each stroke before tying the red ribbon to keep her hair from falling into her round pale face and large eyes. Snow never thought much about how she looked— and that day wasn't any different—but she thought it was sweet the king always said she hadn't changed over the years. Though she had to admit she did have a few more lines around her eyes and mouth when she smiled, which was most of the time. Snow was so accustomed to seeing her mother's face in her mirror that it was strange to see her own. She hadn't realized how much she took her mother's company for granted. How lonely she would feel without her. Especially now that her children were grown and living in their own kingdoms and her beloved was away on a diplomatic mission.

You look beautiful, my bird. You always do.

Snow White looked up with a gleaming smile at the refection of her mother in the mirror. "Momma! Where were you? I have to tell you about my dream!"

"I know your dreams, my darling. I've been trying to find the Dark Fairy. I have to warn her," the old queen Grimhilde replied.

"Is she the Dragon Witch?" Snow White asked.

Grimhilde laughed. "Yes, my bird, the very one."

"Is your old story coming true, then?" Snow asked, confused. "I don't understand!"

"I'm not sure I do, either, darling. The story I told you so many years ago was in a book your cousins gave to me. I think they may have written it. And I'd very much like to see it now. Do you have it somewhere among your things, by chance?"

Snow White knew exactly where it was. It was in a place she didn't like going. "It's not in my chambers. It's in one of the trunks in the attic, packed away with the rest of your possessions."

"Are you brave enough to go up there alone, my bird? It's very important that you do."

CHAPTER VII

THE FAIRY ACADEMY

One morning, Maleficent was messily munching on a blueberry scone while tossing crumbs to her favorite crow, Opal. It had been more than a year since Nanny had found the tiny Maleficent and taken her into her home. She had given the girl time to become comfortable in her new surroundings before bringing up school, and now Nanny decided it was time to broach the subject. "It's time to think about your education, my darling. You must learn your fairy magic."

"But I'm not a fairy!" Maleficent protested.

"Of course you are, my dear. What in the

Fairylands gave you the idea you aren't a fairy?" Nanny asked.

"I don't know."

"Right! You don't know! And that's exactly my point. There are many things you don't know, and the only way you will learn them is by going to school!"

"But . . ."

"But nothing," Nanny said firmly. "Don't worry about those flighty featherhead fairies. If they say or do one thing that makes you sad, you tell me. That goes for your instructors, as well. And I will be there, my dear. Every hour of every single day, I'll be at your disposal without fail."

"Will you?" Maleficent asked.

"Yes, my dearest. I am the headmistress, after all."

So Maleficent's education began. It started out slowly and wasn't quite what Maleficent expected. She learned the properties of magical plants and how to brew potions, and she easily mastered enchanting inanimate objects to do mundane tasks. But Maleficent could tell that her teachers didn't like her, even though she was brighter and more advanced than any of the other students. They didn't show her the affection or care they showed the other students. That didn't bother Maleficent, except that she often found herself without much to do.

During flying lessons, while other fairies learned how to use their wings properly, she sat by herself and read books she had found tucked away on Nanny's bookshelves. Nanny had thought the books were hidden where Maleficent couldn't find them. They contained the sort of magic Maleficent had expected to learn in fairy classes. So, guided by her books, Maleficent began to practice her own magic.

Maleficent quickly realized that she could teach herself almost anything she wanted to do by reading a book. There wasn't a subject that didn't fascinate her. She coveted her time alone after school in her tree house, where she could read, and she'd often share her findings with her crows. Maleficent had decorated her tree house with the various things her crows and ravens brought to her. She found it interesting that some crows were drawn to particular items. Opal had a fondness for brightly colored pieces of sea glass, shiny buttons, and beautiful beads like those found on a fancy ball gown. While some of Maleficent's birds brought her herbs for her spells, others brought colorful feathers, random teacups, brass bells, and anything else that struck their fancy. She loved spending time with her crows and taught them everything she learned on the subjects of bird lore and magic. She started to teach them how to open their minds so she could see through their eyes when they traveled, and how to communicate with other creatures to learn about their lands. Maleficent hadn't known that so many other lands existed until her crows told her stories of the different realms that stretched in every direction into what seemed like a never-ending eternity. She felt lucky to have her pets, especially in light of how little in common she had with her schoolmates. The other fairies were incessantly buzzing around each other, complimenting one another for the silliest of things.

"Merryweather, your wings look lovely today!" was something Maleficent heard far too often in the classroom while she was trying to brew nightshade in her cauldron. The other fairies in Maleficent's class seemed to defer to Merryweather. In Maleficent's opinion, Merryweather was a rather unremarkable fairy and was far too bossy. Nevertheless, she seemed to be the favorite of all the instructors, which made her all the more impossible to deal with. Despite her penchant for bullying and her inflated sense of self, Merryweather was a good student. She spent her breaks in the courtyard studying and tutoring the other students. Maleficent thought she and the fairy could be friends—if Merryweather didn't dislike her so much. There wasn't a day that went by when Maleficent wasn't teased or looked down on by her classmates. If she was trying to study or work at a spell, her classmates would mock her for having to walk from her cauldron to the pantry and back instead of flying. They'd whisper nasty things as they fluttered by, like "Wingless freak!" or "Ogre horns!"

One afternoon in class, Fauna, one of Merryweather's best friends, raised her hand to ask a question. Fauna was a sweet-faced fairy dressed in green. She seemed too nervous to ask Miss Petal the question when she called on her, but Merryweather nudged her on. "Miss Petal, wouldn't it be more . . . uh . . . *pleasant* if Maleficent wore something to cover her disgusting ogre horns in class?" Fauna said in a small voice.

Maleficent looked up from her bubbling cauldron to see what the teacher would say. The teacher grew scarlet under Maleficent's steely gaze. "I daresay it would be more pleasant, and less . . . uh . . . distracting. Perhaps I will say something to her guardian."

All the students were giggling at Miss Petal's reply when the class was interrupted by the unexpected arrival of the headmistress, who shot the teacher and students a scathing look. "I daresay

Maleficent would find it more pleasing if you all had your wings snipped! She wouldn't have you buzzing around her head while she's trying to work her spell, that's for certain! But you don't see *her* vocalizing her every daydream, do you?"

Maleficent grew white with embarrassment, a striking difference from her usual green complexion. "I never . . . I didn't . . ." she stammered.

"And who could blame you if you did?" Nanny looked at the students as she continued. "You're a shameful bunch, the lot of you. Disgusting horns indeed! Did you ever stop to think there are creatures in this world who might find *wings* disgusting? Have you not yet realized that the sun doesn't rise and set by fairy standards? There are other creatures in this world, dear ones! Beautiful, lovely, and powerful creatures that don't look like me or you! You'd do well to remember that, Fauna! All of you would!"

The fairies didn't pay much attention to the One of Legends when she went on about such things. She didn't make sense. *Everyone* knew fairy wings were beautiful! How could anyone in all the lands ever consider them otherwise? The One of Legends was much too serious. She wasn't at all like her sister. The Fairy Godmother was proud of her wings, sang beautiful songs, and taught the best class of all: wish granting! None of the fairies could wait until they were old enough for wish-granting class.

As far as Merryweather was concerned, that was the highest honor for fairy students. The fairies knew in their hearts that Maleficent would never make it that far. Not that she had much of a chance with Merryweather, Fauna, and Flora being up for wish-granting status in the same year as her. The Fairy Godmother herself had said she felt there was a very good chance Flora, Fauna, and Merryweather would be awarded status. And since wish-granting status was bestowed on only three students in any graduating class, it seemed silly for Maleficent—or any other student, for that matter—to pursue it as her fairy calling. Besides, there were many other important things a fairy could do upon graduating from the academy.

Giving Merryweather and her friends a nasty look, Nanny walked out the door. Once she left, the class erupted in a storm of protest. "What does she see in Maleficent?" Merryweather yelled.

"She can't even fly!" one fairy screamed.

"You're not even a fairy. You don't belong here. Go back to Hades!" said another.

Maleficent sat rigid and afraid. She didn't understand why all the fairies hated her so much. Was it really her horns? Or was something terribly wrong with her? Was she evil?

She didn't *feel* evil.

She felt like everyone else. At least, she thought she did. Come to think of it, she didn't really know how everyone else felt. Maybe she *was* evil.

My parents must have known I was evil. That's why they left me in the crow tree. They wanted me to die.

As the taunting continued, Maleficent was aware of something swelling up inside her, a horrible burning sensation she didn't like. She felt like she was slowly catching fire from the inside, as if a flame was struggling to get out of her. Before she knew it, her entire body was engulfed in a stifling green blaze.

Maleficent heard the other students screaming. But before she could process what was happening, she found herself alone in her tree house, confused as to how she had gotten there. She shook uncontrollably with rage and fear, crying harder than she ever had before. The shrieks of the other fairies were still echoing in her ears when Nanny appeared with a worried look on her face.

"I didn't . . . I didn't mean it!" Maleficent stammered.

"You didn't mean what, dear?" Nanny asked.

"To hurt them . . ." Maleficent cried.

"You didn't hurt them," Nanny said reassuringly. "You completed a magnificent travel charm. It's a difficult spell that's way beyond your grade level. I'm very impressed!"

"But they were screaming!"

"Oh, yes, well, that's young fairies for you. Dramatic and high-strung! You're a smart girl, Maleficent. I'm sure you know this already." Nanny paused for a moment and then continued. "I couldn't be more pleased at how different you are from those fools, Maleficent. I truly couldn't. Had you been an ordinary fairy living in that hollowed-out tree, I think I would have probably passed you by!"

"If I was an ordinary fairy, I wouldn't have been left in the tree."

Nanny nodded vigorously. "Too right! That's one of the main reasons I don't care for my own ilk. And why I don't display my wings. Fairies can be a hateful bunch."

Maleficent smiled, her tears subsiding, as she listened to Nanny. She wanted to hug her. She wanted to tell her she loved her for everything she was saying, but she didn't want to interrupt her.

"Oh, they don't realize how hateful they are. They think they're full of magic and light and all things good! Like sugar and honey comes out of their . . . Well, you get my point."

Maleficent laughed.

"Well, isn't that a rare sight? In the years we've been together, I don't think I have ever seen you laugh." Nanny paused for a moment, deep in thought. "Hmmm, it all makes sense now."

"What? What makes sense?" Maleficent asked.

"You're seven. Seven!"

"What's so special about being seven?"

"Seven is a very special age for fairies. Especially for fairies who aren't like the others. Fairies like you and me, who are more like witches than fairies. Fairies who aren't content with fairy magic and fairy life and understand there are other wonderful forms of magic in this world. Seven is just the start of your adventure. And I think we need to celebrate! Now, tell me all about that travel charm. I want to hear about how you learned it. You're a fascination to me, Maleficent. You're further in your schooling than anyone in your class. And if that stack of books of mine you have hidden away is any indication of the style of magic you intend to employ, we have a lot of work to do. I think you're up to the task. I really do! You know what? I think it might be time to take you out of that school. I can't have your spirit and potential squelched by those dimwits. Let them fumble with their silly fairy magic. Let them spend their days complimenting each other's wings. You have real magic to learn. Important magic."

Important magic. Those words echoed in Maleficent's ears and filled her with confidence.

That was how it was with Nanny. A flurry of encouraging words and love thrown at Maleficent from every direction. Nanny never missed an opportunity to heap love upon the girl. And if Maleficent sometimes felt overwhelmed by the magnitude of Nanny's affection, or occasionally grew stiff at Nanny's touch, it wasn't because she didn't like the attention. Maleficent loved Nanny, more deeply than she expected she might.

She just wasn't used to *being* loved.

"Well, I'm going to bake you a marvelous cake for dessert," Nanny said, clapping her hands excitedly. "I want to hear all about this travel charm and how you managed it. I really am impressed!"

Maleficent knew that Nanny was being sincere. She never said anything she didn't mean like the other fairies. It was hard to tell Nanny was a fairy at all. Maleficent wondered if Nanny had also had a hard time growing up in the Fairylands, being so un-fairylike and having as a sister the famous Fairy Godmother.

"No, dear, that part wasn't hard at all!" Nanny said, reading her thoughts. "They don't call me the One of Legends for nothing!"

That was one of the best nights of Maleficent's childhood—spent eating cake with Nanny and telling her about the travel charm. Describing the warm sensation and seeing the awe reflected in Nanny's eyes when she explained it in every detail, just as Nanny had wanted.

"You did exactly the right thing, my dear! If someone is treating you poorly or you feel yourself becoming angry and you start to feel that warm sensation, you use that charm. Go straight to your tree house, or straight to me and your crows. You just think of us, and you will find yourself with us before you know it. Promise me, dear, you will do what Nanny tells you."

"Of course, Nanny." Maleficent wished she had

Nanny's power to read minds. She often wondered what Nanny was thinking. Was that concern in her eyes? Had something about Maleficent's story upset her?

"No, my dear. What you see is pride! I couldn't be prouder of you. You've made me very happy today, my darling. Very happy indeed."

CHAPTER VIII

THE BIRD
IN THE ATTIC

Snow White sat alone in the attic among her mother's old belongings, remembering how things were long ago, in the time before her stepmother died and became the mother Snow White had always wanted her to be. Snow understood why her mother didn't want to go up there. Those possessions reminded the old queen of the period when she had sequestered herself years earlier—the time when she had gone mad with grief and plotted to kill her own stepdaughter. Snow tried to compartmentalize her mother into three different women: the mother she had now, the mother who had loved her when she was very young, and the mother who had tried to kill her. Snow knew it wasn't her mother's fault. The queen had been tormented by her own father, heartbroken by the loss of her husband, and bewitched by the witch triplets. Snow had made the various versions of her mother over the years into imaginary dolls—dolls she kept locked away in a trunk in this room. Dolls she never wanted to play with or see.

Dolls imbued with pain and covered in dust.

Snow liked the mother she had now. She had no reason to revisit the others. Even the recollection of her sweet mother from her early childhood brought Snow heartache, because she knew all those terrible days that followed her father's death would come tumbling down like an avalanche, reminding her of how grief had destroyed that mother.

Yes, she liked to focus on the woman she loved dearly and depended on now. But she couldn't look at her mother's things without bringing those dolls into the light, taking them into her hands and dusting them off as she replayed the timeline of her life. Those dolls, those mothers marked the passing of beautiful yet terrifying times.

With quiet, tentative steps, Snow went to one of the wooden chests that contained the artifacts of her tortured childhood. It creaked painfully as she opened it, like a warning. The book of fairy tales she was looking for was sitting beneath a small wooden box with a carving of a dagger piercing a heart. Something about the box sent chills into Snow's own heart. She didn't want to know what was in it. She didn't want to see the pain on her mother's face if she were to ask her about the box, so it would have to remain a mystery. It was enough that she was up there alone, knowing her mother was waiting for her. Knowing each moment that passed was a pain in her mother's heart.

Snow suddenly felt like she had when she was very small. In the old castle where she had grown up, there had been a hallway that had always frightened her. There was no particular reason for her fear, aside from the fact that the hallway was always rather dark. Snow's imagination had conjured up all sorts of nightmares living in the shadows. But she used to have to walk down that hallway every day to reach the classroom where she met her tutor. Some days, she was so afraid that she would run, even though she knew her governess, Verona, would scold her for her unladylike behavior. Snow hadn't cared. She had felt compelled to run for safety even in the bright light of day. Snow White felt like that now. She tried not to look at what else was in the chest. She tried to suppress the pain surging through her heart. Snow removed the book as quickly as she could, trying not to disturb the other contents. Then she slammed the chest closed, causing dust to cascade into the air, where it glittered in the sunlight streaming through the little attic window. She looked at it for a moment, dazzled by the brilliance of something seemingly mundane. Snow mused about how something usually so ugly could turn into something quite beautiful. And she remembered her mother. Her mother's transformation. Her mother's beauty.

And suddenly, she wasn't as frightened.

Chapter IX

Her Important Magic

As the years passed, Nanny could tell the coldness inside Maleficent was thawing. Maleficent wasn't sure if it was from Nanny's love or the thing inside her that had been growing for some time—the terrible burning feeling she sometimes felt when she was angry or sad. She tried to banish it from her mind and focus on her magic. Her important magic, which she studied at every opportunity. On Nanny's bookshelf, she had found several tomes written by the odd sisters, three witches named Lucinda, Ruby, and Martha. Their pages were filled with all sorts of dark magic that intrigued Maleficent. One of the spells was particularly interesting to her. It called for a smattering of herbs along with hair from the witch's own head and instructions to be written in ink on a tiny slip of parchment. These ingredients had to be fed to a very large bullfrog, which the witch would command to find her victim. The bullfrog would then crawl into a sleeping person's mouth and live in their throat, waiting on orders from the witch by means of telepathy. Maleficent had to look up what *telepathy* meant. When she did, she finally had a word for something she had observed in Nanny: the ability to read minds and communicate without speaking. From what Maleficent read in the book, she gathered that the gruesome spell was terrifying for the victim. The witch could command the person to do whatever she liked. The bullfrog would come out only at night, while the host slept, to report its findings to the witch, and then it would squeeze itself back into the victim's mouth before morning. The victim was aware of something living in their throat but was unable to say anything about it.

The book also had a variation of the spell in which the witch would take something personal from the victim she wished to command, instead of using a frog. It could be anything, really: a teacup, a hairbrush, or a ring. And it seemed some witches collected such items should there ever be an occasion in which they needed them. Maleficent didn't want to do such dark spells. They seemed rather ghastly and repulsive to her, actually. She just liked reading and learning about them. Maleficent also loved reading the lyrical and often hilarious notations in the odd sisters' books. They were quickly becoming her favorite spell casters and her favorite witches.

Maleficent liked knowing things. It gave her power. It gave her confidence. The more she read and learned, the less afraid she was of the other fairies. She had a deep sense of pride that while the other fairies were learning how to enchant broomsticks, she was learning valuable charms and spells she could use when she finally ventured out of the Fairylands. Maleficent was learning real magic.

That was most exciting of all.

CHAPTER X

THE ODD
SISTERS' BOOK

Snow White sat on a lovely red velvet chair that she had brought very close to an ornate gold-framed mirror. She held the book of fairy tales her mother had once read to her on her lap, flipping through the pages so her mother could see.

"All of our stories are in there!" Grimhilde said.

Snow turned to the last page of the Dragon Witch's story, looking at it in horror. "Will this happen to your friend Maleficent?"

"I don't know, my dear, but I need to warn her." Grimhilde's reflection flickered as it sometimes did when she was worried. "I haven't been able to reach her in any of her mirrors. You must send word to

Morningstar Castle. I think she will arrive there shortly."

"I don't understand why you're friends with her after what she's done to Aurora," Snow White said, shaking her head.

"She has her reasons, my dear," Grimhilde replied. "Reasons that are not mine to share with you or anyone else. I have been her friend and confidant for many years, Snow. I can't turn my back on her now just because we don't agree with her choices. Perhaps I will be able to talk her out of hurting the girl and save her from sharing my fate."

Snow considered that for a moment. "But I don't understand. This book was written long before Maleficent ever considered putting the princess to sleep. How is it that everything that has been written in it has come to pass?" Snow turned to another page. "And look! Here is a section about you and me! It details everything, even you coming into the mirror and being my protector. How is that possible?"

Grimhilde looked concerned. "I don't know. Our

story wasn't there when last I read this book to you. The book may be writing itself like a history, or perhaps the sisters were able to see into the future and wrote down their prophecies."

"What if it's a spell? What if the book is enchanted and anything that's written within its pages comes true?" Snow asked.

"Spellbound!" the old queen gasped. The thought sent chills through Snow. "If that is true, then no one will be able to protect those sisters from my vengeance! I've long accepted that I chose my own path down the road of regret. But if it was all designed by those sisters, if it was written by them, and I was simply their puppet, then there will be Hades to pay!"

"Mother, no!" Snow pleaded. "I will write to Morningstar to warn them about the book. Now please, promise me you won't hurt anyone."

"I can't do that, my darling. I'm sorry. If they are the reason I tried to kill you, then no power will be great enough to save the odd sisters from my wrath!"

CHAPTER XI

THE DARK FAIRY'S GIFT

Many years had passed since Nanny had taken the young Maleficent out of school so she could focus on her own brand of magic, giving her room to explore and experience the world of magic outside fairy lore.

Maleficent had changed considerably from the little creature she had been when Nanny found her in the hollow of the crow tree. Though none of the other fairies would admit it, Maleficent was remarkably beautiful. Nanny had always known Maleficent would grow into her features. But beauty didn't matter much to Maleficent. Her concerns lay elsewhere.

One bright sunny morning, she and Nanny were sitting at the kitchen table. They were sipping their tea out of black-and-silver teacups and enjoying the black-currant scones Nanny had baked earlier that morning. Nanny could tell Maleficent had something she wanted to announce. Maleficent was always making declarations of some sort, about a spell she had just mastered or a new subject she wanted to tackle. But this particular announcement took Nanny by surprise.

"Nanny, I think I would like to sit for the fairy exams," Maleficent finally said.

Nanny cast an uneasy eye on her daughter. "Why? Your magic far surpasses fairy magic, so why bother?"

"Because I want to master all manners of magic! And I don't want to give those flighty fairies an excuse to mock me. Besides, I've perfected my means of teleporting from one place to the next. Really, there's no reason I shouldn't become a wish-granting fairy if I chose to be one," Maleficent argued.

"Do you want to be one, my dear?" Nanny asked. "I never imagined you would be inclined to such things."

"Why shouldn't I? I am a fairy, after all, and I shouldn't shrink from any school of magic simply because my old classmates were unkind," Maleficent reasoned. "Besides, I've been practicing, and I think I'm ready for exams. I will be eligible to take the exam tomorrow, if I recall correctly."

"You do recall correctly, my dear, as always, and without fail," Nanny said with a sigh. "And I don't doubt you're ready for the exam. You could have taken it when you were ten. Although now that you're turning sixteen, it *is* the proper time to sit for the exam." Nanny seemed lost in her thoughts for a moment. "If you wish, you may take the exam. Far be it from me to hold you back from furthering your education. Since most of your education has been either self-taught or taught by me, it's not official. It will do you well to have a certificate to prove you have completed your fairy lessons. Though I thought we would spend your sixteenth birthday in some other fashion."

Maleficent smiled. "Did you hear that, Diablo? I'm going to sit for my fairy exams!"

Diablo flew into the room, cawing in celebration, his wings outstretched.

Nanny loved seeing Maleficent that happy. And Maleficent's relationship with Diablo, a new acquisition for her aviary, made Nanny smile. Though Maleficent still held a very special place for her crows, she loved her raven, Diablo, who never seemed to leave her side for very long.

"Come on, Diablo! Let's practice wish granting in the garden! I need to be perfect for my exams tomorrow!"

Nanny chuckled to herself as the two rushed into the garden. It had been a joke between the two of them that Maleficent had decided to name the raven Diablo. It was their way of poking fun at the fairies for having given Maleficent such a menacing name.

Nanny had just stood to put another kettle on

the fire when there was a knock at the door. "Come in!" she yelled in a cheery voice. It was her sister, the Fairy Godmother. "Ah, come in, Sister. I just put some water on for tea. Would you like to join me in a cup?"

"Yes, please," the Fairy Godmother replied as she stepped into the cottage.

Nanny took a cup from the cupboard that she knew her sister would fancy—a pretty opalescent teacup that reflected different muted colors depending on the light. Nanny placed the cup and teapot on the table, pretending she didn't know why her sister had come by for a visit. The truth was her sister never came over. They weren't the sort of sisters who met for tea, but Nanny made a pretense that they were. Secretly, she wished they were that sort of sisters.

The Fairy Godmother cleared her throat. "I'm here because I was passing by and I noticed Maleficent practicing wish granting in the front garden."

"Indeed she is," Nanny said as she poured the tea

and put out the sugar cubes for her sister. The Fairy Godmother's normally pleasant face had contorted into a crooked frown.

"What's troubling you, Sister?" Nanny asked, pretending she hadn't already guessed.

"Is Maleficent turning sixteen tomorrow?" the Fairy Godmother asked.

Nanny narrowed her eyes at her sister's question. "Yes, she is, Sister."

The Fairy Godmother pursed her lips. "How can you be sure? We don't know when she was born."

Nanny smiled thinly, much in the same way her sister did when she was saying something unpleasant. "You know our powers work differently. I can see time and can visit those times. I know tomorrow is her birthday."

"Well, sixteen or not, as headmistress you know a fairy cannot sit for exams without first successfully completing all the classes necessary to qualify her for the honor," the Fairy Godmother reminded Nanny.

"And as headmistress, I can make exceptions when I choose," Nanny said. "I would make the same case for any fairy who had the same extensive knowledge as Maleficent. She has learned everything necessary to qualify her for the exams and more. I say she sits for them!"

The Fairy Godmother stood up from her chair, slamming her hands on the table. "I don't understand what you see in this girl. Our powers may work differently, but I've seen her future in my dreams. She will bring you nothing but heartache! I've seen it. And so have you!"

"Time is not fixed, Sister," Nanny said, rebuking her. "The future especially! You know this. She deserves a chance. And she certainly deserves the opportunity to have a future, which she wouldn't have had if I hadn't come back and taken her in!"

"Not this again! I won't have you condemning me for the rest of our many long lifetimes with this nonsense," the Fairy Godmother snapped.

"Nonsense? You left her in the cold! You left her alone with the crows. You didn't care if she lived or died."

"It's useless talking to you about this. You won't

see reason. She is *evil*! You know that she is! Bring her for the exam if you wish. I can't do anything to stop you. But the decision to pass or fail her remains mine."

Nanny shook her head. "You are so fairy-minded. If it doesn't fit inside your ideal version of the world, if it stands out in any way, then you want it ripped from your view. Maleficent is like a black orchid in a field of pink peonies. You're incapable of letting the orchid flourish. You would remove it because it looks out of place."

"You love Maleficent because she's an orchid."

"And you hate her because I do!" Nanny was getting angry. Angry at her sister for not being the sister she had always wanted and for being so closed-minded. But most of all, she was angry because she was worried her sister might be right. *No! Stop it. She's not right. You've raised a beautiful, intelligent, gifted young woman. You've given her every opportunity and she will make you proud.*

"Keep telling yourself that. Maybe one day

you will actually believe it," the Fairy Godmother snapped, leaving before drinking her tea. She was angry—a feeling she hated. The Fairy Godmother liked herself always to be seen as happy and good, but that ideal version of her was never reflected at her in her sister's eyes.

With a steely look, the Fairy Godmother passed Maleficent on her way out of the yard.

"Why does she hate me so much?" Maleficent asked as she went back inside the cottage.

"She's just jealous, my dear. Don't you worry. Now help me get ready for dinner. We're having guests to celebrate your birthday," Nanny said in her usual calming tone. "Now, where's your pet?"

Maleficent looked down as if she had been caught at something she was sure Nanny would disapprove of. "I sensed the presence of powerful witches in the area and I sent him to see who they were."

Nanny's mouth pinched and shifted to the left side of her face, as it often did when she was per- plexed. "My dear, why didn't you just ask me? I could have told you it was the odd sisters, on their way here. I've asked them to join us for dinner this evening."

Maleficent was shocked. "The odd sisters? The authors of all those spell books? They're coming here?"

"Yes, I thought they would be a lovely surprise for your birthday! I know how well you love their books of magic. They are old friends of mine and I haven't had them over for quite some time. I figured this was a lovely opportunity for a visit. I had thought to cancel after you told me you planned to take the exam. I know my sister won't like their being here, but the odd sisters insisted. I just hope my sister doesn't take her frustrations out on you tomorrow when she's grading your exam."

Maleficent wondered how Nanny had been able to send the odd sisters an owl while her sister was there.

"She sent us the message telepathically, of course, little one!" a trio of voices called from outside.

Startled, Maleficent jumped back. Three women

appeared at the door. They were Lucinda, Ruby, and Martha. Identical triplets. The odd sisters. The authors of some of her favorite spell books! She had never imagined being able to meet them. And she wondered why Nanny had never told her she knew the famous witches. Maleficent looked over the odd sisters. She hadn't expected them to be identical, but there they stood, a trio of beautiful women. All of them had pitch-black hair and overly large black eyes lined with black coal. Their tiny little rosebud mouths were colored with red lip paint, which was striking against their very pale skin. Their skin was almost too perfect, and they looked like porcelain dolls. Everything about them matched, down to their hairstyles and their dark green voluminous dresses, embroidered with rusty autumn leaves that seemed to change color depending on the light. They wore their hair in intricate buns with green and orange gems woven into their springy curls. Maleficent had never seen such beautiful women in her life, and she hadn't expected her favorite spell casters to be so lovely.

"Thank you, my dear," the triplet in the middle said. She seemed to be the eldest.

"Come in! Come in!" Nanny said excitedly as she pulled out more cups for their guests. "Let's sit down and have some tea. I would like you to get to know my daughter, Maleficent. It has been far too long since I've seen you, and introductions are far overdue."

"Oh, we know all about Maleficent," Lucinda said.

"We watch her in our mirror!" said Martha.

Ruby hushed them. "Shhh! Don't tell them our secrets!"

Maleficent laughed. She had never met anyone like the women, and she'd instantly fallen in love with them. It seemed they were mind readers, like Nanny. Maleficent was used to being in the company of someone who knew her thoughts, so it didn't bother her at all.

"We love you, too! Happy birthday, Maleficent! Happy birthday! Tomorrow is an extraordinary day!" sang all three sisters. "Sixteen is a very special age. Very special indeed. We wouldn't miss it, my dear!"

"So, One of Legends, is your sister still up to her old tricks?" Lucinda asked as she intently watched Nanny set out the teacups. Nanny smiled to herself, knowing one of the witches would slip a cup into her pocket, as they did almost every time they visited.

"What does she mean by 'old tricks,' Nanny?" Maleficent asked.

Nanny gave the sisters a sideways look. "Nothing, my dear. It's nothing."

"Don't lie to the child!" Lucinda screeched.

"Never helps to tell lies . . ." Ruby sang.

"Never helps!" Martha chimed in. "You can't protect her forever, Granny!"

Nanny laughed at the "granny" remark but didn't take it personally. She knew Martha was just being silly. Besides, she was much older than even the odd sisters probably suspected. "Come now, ladies. No one is lying to the girl," Nanny said, trying to calm the odd sisters.

"She's becoming a woman tomorrow! Sixteen! Sixteen! Sixteen!" The sisters were all chiming in as if in a chaotic choir. The rhythmic canter of their voices was intoxicating to Maleficent.

"Protect me from what?" Maleficent asked.

"From the truth, my dear! The truth!" The sisters laughed so loudly Maleficent's crows scattered from her tree house. Their caws echoed throughout the Fairylands.

"Ha! That will cause those simpletons a fright!" the odd sisters cried.

"What? My crows?" asked Maleficent, taking in everything about the sisters she could. She examined their eyes, their expressions, the way they moved their hands. The women were a marvel to her.

"Oh, yes! Everyone knows crows are evil," the sisters said, and laughed.

"Oh, stop this foolishness!" Nanny cried as she poured the tea. "They're laughing at the fairies' expense, of course, Maleficent, not yours."

Lucinda seemed to be scrutinizing Maleficent even more closely than Maleficent had been scrutinizing the sisters. "You have yourself a smart young witch here, my friend. I think she was already aware of our intent."

"I'm a fairy, not a witch," Maleficent said.

"Oh, you are a witch, my dearie! A truer witch than we've ever met!" Ruby exclaimed.

"Your powers may even surpass those of the One of Legends someday!" Martha squeaked.

"Perhaps sooner than she expects," Lucinda said somberly.

"But Nanny . . . Nanny is a fairy, too," Maleficent insisted.

"You may have both been *born* fairies, but you are witches at heart! You do *real magic*!" Lucinda cried.

The sisters laughed so hard Maleficent thought the windows of their little cottage would shatter. "Besides, what is a fairy without wings if not a witch, little one?" the sisters sang in unison, making Maleficent smile.

Nanny loved to see her girl so happy but was distracted by a sharp burning smell. "Oh! I almost forgot dinner!"

The witches laughed as Nanny rushed to the oven in a panic. "You didn't burn the dinner, did you, Granny?" asked Ruby, making her sisters laugh even harder.

"No, I didn't, thank the gods," said Nanny. "Come now, let's eat."

✤ ✤ ✤ ✤

During dinner, they all discussed the exams that were to take place the following day. The witches were careful not to do or say anything that would give the Fairy Godmother cause to think Maleficent had cheated in any way.

"Oh, I think Circe is going to love pretending to be a princess in need tomorrow!" Ruby said as she picked at her food, pushing it around her plate.

"Circe?" asked Maleficent.

"She's the odd sisters' much younger sister. She will be playing the part of a charge for the examination. We usually ask friends to bring their sons and daughters or little brothers and sisters for the exam. Since the odd sisters were already coming to visit for your birthday, I thought they could bring Circe to the exam. None of the students have ever met Circe, so it would make the exam experience more realistic," Nanny explained.

"Is she my age?" Maleficent asked.

Martha shook her head. "No, dear, much younger, but I daresay one day when the age difference no longer matters, you would be good friends, if everything—"

"If everything doesn't go to plan!" Lucinda said, finishing Martha's prediction.

"If the stars do not align!" sang Ruby.

"Oh, yes! You may be friends! I see friendship!" Martha added.

"Or disaster," they said together in a strange chorus.

Nanny shot the odd sisters a dangerous look. They blinked back with worried expressions.

"Let's hope the stars do not align," Nanny said sternly.

Maleficent noticed the strange exchange but pretended it hadn't happened.

"Well, I wish she was here. I would like to meet

her!" Maleficent said. She was excited by the idea of meeting a witch closer to her in age.

"And give the Scary Godmother a reason to disqualify you?" Lucinda asked.

"I think not!" Martha said.

"Oh, no, my dear!" Ruby insisted.

"No, no, no!" screeched the odd sisters together.

Maleficent was amused by the sisters' outburst. "Ah, I see. If she joined us for dinner, the Fairy Godmother would think we had colluded to help me pass the exam."

"Yes! Although she's not allowed to be your charge tomorrow!"

"Oh, no! That wouldn't do!"

"Because we are friends with your nanny!"

"Hades forbid!"

"She will join us for cake tomorrow!"

"Circe loves birthday cake!"

"You're turning sixteen!"

"Sixteen!"

"We will all eat cake if the stars are not right!"

Nanny changed the subject. "Darling, there's

something else you should know. Not all the stand-in charges are real. Some of them are merely projections, like ghosts. They are trickier than the stand-in charges, because they are based on real people from history. Sometimes they are from the future and sometimes they're from the past. . . ."

But Maleficent wasn't listening.

"What is it, dear? What has you so distracted?" Nanny asked.

"Diablo—he never came back after I sent him out earlier today. . . ." Maleficent said. She had been enjoying the company of Nanny and the odd sisters so much she had almost forgotten about Diablo.

"To spy on us, you mean?" the odd sisters asked. "Oh, we saw him. He's a good pet, my dear, but he needs to practice his spying skills a bit more before you send him off on such errands." The sisters laughed some more.

"I'm sure he's fine, little one. Just taking the opportunity to fly about," Ruby said, cackling.

"Our cat, Pflanze, does the same," Martha said, laughing even harder. "Oh, she doesn't fly, mind you! She slinks, she slinks and slinks and slinks away! She's beastly, sometimes staying out for days at a time, never bothering to tell us where she's going or where she's been!"

Lucinda agreed with her sisters. "I wouldn't worry about it, dear. I'm sure your little devil is fine."

Nanny put her hand on Maleficent's and smiled. "I know you're enjoying our company, dear one, but you'd better get to bed. Your exam is rather early tomorrow morning."

"Can I sleep in my tree house, in case Diablo comes back?"

Nanny nodded. "Yes, just do not to stay up all night waiting for him."

Everyone stood to hug Maleficent.

"Good night, Maleficent!"

"Good night!"

"We love you, Maleficent! Happy birthday."

Maleficent couldn't remember ever being happier. She had a wonderful mother in Nanny, and now three amazing witches in her life who loved her. Her sixteenth birthday was bound to be better than she had hoped.

If only she weren't so worried about Diablo, everything would be perfect. Everything would be all right.

CHAPTER XII

The Many Lifetimes
of Nanny

As Circe and Nanny walked back to Morningstar
Castle together, Nanny's mind was still occupied
by memories of Maleficent. Nanny wondered if
Maleficent knew she was at Morningstar. Nanny
knew Maleficent could feel the vibrations of power
moving in the world. She could sense where to
find a witch, but she could not discern exactly who
the witch was. Still, Nanny had to wonder why
Maleficent was coming to Morningstar at all. Was
she coming to see the odd sisters? Or was she coming to confront her?

"She'll arrive soon," Nanny told Circe as they
reached the castle. They each gave a little nod to

Hudson, Morningstar Castle's head butler, as they made their way through the vestibule and into the morning room. "Why do you think she's making the trip here?"

"I think Maleficent has come because of what happened to Ursula," Circe said.

"Maleficent had no love for Ursula," Nanny reminded her.

"True, but she had to have felt the great surge of power in the realms. She probably wants to know what caused it," Circe pointed out.

Nanny thought about it. "She *did* warn your sisters not to trust Ursula. She's probably here to lord it over them."

Whatever Maleficent's reason, Nanny felt safe having Circe on her side.

"Of course I am on your side. I love you," Circe said, reading Nanny's thoughts.

Nanny looked at Circe with a sad smile. "Let's hope that never changes. I've had young girls tell me that and they later regretted it."

Circe didn't think that was true. She was sure

Nanny felt that way only because the daughter she loved most no longer loved her. And the loss of Maleficent, the loss of her daughter's love, made Nanny feel like she was a disappointment to all those around her.

"I've never regretted loving you!" Princess Tulip said, bounding into the morning room and giving Nanny a kiss on the cheek.

Nanny suddenly felt very happy having the two wonderful young ladies with her. It reminded her of a time when her adopted daughter had loved her just as much as Circe and Tulip did now. Nanny's stomach lurched at the thought of her seeing Maleficent and having their inevitable confrontation. So many years had passed since they had seen each other. And their last encounter had been devastating.

"Tulip, my dear, can I get you to do some research for me?" Nanny asked, distracting herself from her thoughts. "Could you please go to the library and look up any creatures in Morningstar that are plant- or earth-based? Other than the Tree Lords and Cyclopean Giants, of course, since you have already read everything there is to know about them."

Tulip looked at Nanny suspiciously. "Are you trying to get rid of me?"

Nanny shook her head. "No, my dear, it's very important. I know this subject interests you, and I happen to be in great need of the information."

Circe could see confusion on Tulip's face. "I'll go with you to the library and explain. She's no longer a child, Nanny! She deserves to know what's happening," Circe said as Nanny shot her a concerned look.

As Circe and Tulip headed out of the room, Circe turned. "I'll be right back. Don't worry; I'm not leaving you alone for long."

Nanny's head was spinning and her heart raced. Reliving one's many lifetimes—for truly, that was what Nanny had lived—was like a gift that brought only heartache. It was easy to look back on past mistakes and wish better choices had been made. But to remember all past transgressions at once, to have them tumble down in great succession, was like nothing Nanny had ever experienced. Failing her adopted daughter was the gravest mistake of her lifetimes. And now Tulip was caught up in the mess, with her mother and father stuck in the kingdom, enchanted by a sleeping curse. Everything was in ruins. Nanny seemed to be surrounded by nothing but grief and impending disaster. She didn't know where to begin.

But she did. She had already begun.

Tulip was researching the local creatures, old and new. Nanny needed to know if there were any creatures in Morningstar that would pose a threat to Maleficent. And she would have Circe look for a spell that would wake her sisters. The witches' house was still resting on the cliffs by the sea. Surely there was some spell hidden away in their many volumes that could help them.

Circe came back into the room. "I have explained everything to Tulip. She understands and isn't afraid. She's changed so much since I first met her; she's changed a great deal since yesterday. It's wonderful to see her becoming such a remarkable young woman. I'm sure you're proud of her."

Nanny smiled. "I have always been proud of her. I've always seen her as the woman she would become. I never doubted Tulip would someday become the extraordinary young woman I knew she was."

"Did you see who Maleficent would become?" Circe asked.

Nanny nodded. "I did. But I tried to change her future. I tried to steer her in another direction. And in my attempt to save her, I gave her all the tools she needed to become the mistress of all evil."

That was Nanny's greatest failure, although Maleficent likely saw it as Nanny's greatest gift to her. It felt like a knife in her heart to say those words aloud to Circe.

Mistress of all evil.

Nanny knew Circe had been listening to her thoughts as she had recalled her past with Maleficent. She'd made no effort to keep her thoughts secret. Allowing Circe to listen in was far easier and less painful than repeating her mistakes aloud. Nanny knew Circe didn't judge her. Circe was like Nanny:

she could see time in ways others could not. She knew that Nanny had never tried to hurt Maleficent, that Nanny had done all she could to save her little green fairy. Circe was able to rewind and play the recordings of time. Nanny felt Circe likely knew more than she had shared. She probably knew everything. And one day, Nanny thought, Circe might be able to experience all time as one time without going mad. Nanny knew that for now, Circe could visit places in time individually, especially when they were emotionally charged. But it came at a cost: it was exhausting. And Circe needed all her strength to help her sisters. Besides, it was too soon to point Circe on the journey her life would take after she'd settled the matter of her sisters. It was too soon for Nanny to tell Circe of her great destiny, so Nanny was careful to keep these thoughts from Circe until the time was right.

"I will not let you meet Maleficent alone. I just have to do a quick protection spell on the solarium, and I will be right back at your side," Circe said. She gave Nanny a weary look before she kissed her soft, powdery cheek. Circe could feel her heart being pulled in two different directions, between Nanny and her sisters. She knew Nanny could sense it, too. Her sisters' home still sat on the cliffs above Morningstar, and she was certain the answer to waking her sisters lay inside. But her sisters' spell books would have to wait. Her childhood home would still be there when she was ready. Circe couldn't bring herself to leave the castle quite yet. Not while Maleficent's threatening forest of tangling vines drew nearer.

Chapter XIII

Broken Dolls

The odd sisters lay on the floor of the solarium under its massive glass dome. Nanny and Circe had decided to leave them where they had collapsed for fear of harming them, though Circe wondered how they could be harmed any more than they already had been; she couldn't detect any life force in them. To her, they looked like broken, lifeless dolls. Their eyes were still open wide, slightly bulging from their profoundly darkened sockets. She was saddened to see their white cheeks deeply stained with black streaks from long hours of crying before their collapse. Their red lipstick was smudged and settled into the lines around their mouths. It made Circe upset to see her sisters in such a state. Even though she could no longer feel their presence, she knew in her heart that somehow they were still in the world.

Just not in this world.

Muttering a quick incantation, Circe fixed the odd sisters' makeup, curled their onyx ringlets, straightened the feathers in their hair, and righted their beautiful voluminous dresses, made of black silk with a cascade of silver stars, resembling the night sky. If Circe had to delay finding the spell to wake them, the least she could do was give them their dignity. They would have looked peaceful if she just could have closed their eyes. But Circe thought perhaps it was better that they were open. She didn't want to forget her sisters required her help. Circe only wished she could wake them as easily as she had made them look presentable again.

I hope they're okay, wherever they are. Do you think they'll ever wake up? It was Pflanze. The feline had been watching Circe silently as she'd helped her sisters. Seeing her witches motionless on the floor sent a chill through Pflanze's heart. She was afraid she would never speak to them again. Never feel the touch of Ruby's hand or the soft brushing of Lucinda's lips on the top of her head, or feel Martha tugging on her ears.

"Stop fretting, Pflanze. We will find a spell to wake them. I am sure of it." Turning from her sisters, Circe looked at Pflanze. She took in the cat's beauty, dazzled by Pflanze's golden eyes, flecked with green and rimmed with black. They were striking against the vivid patches of orange, black, and white on the cat's face. "You really are a beautiful creature, Pflanze. Keep watch over them. I'll be back."

Are you going to enchant the door? I feel uneasy with my witches so defenseless, especially if Maleficent is on her way.

"Of course. Don't worry," Circe said. She quietly closed the door behind her so as not to disturb her sleeping sisters and their loyal guardian. With a wave of her hand, Circe created a powerful barricade around the room. Only those with a pure heart and noble intentions would be able to open the door. No one who intended to harm the sisters would be able to enter the solarium. And no magic would be strong enough to break the spell—not a spell woven in love for the protection and safety of her beloved sisters.

CHAPTER XIV

CONVERGENCE

Owls, crows, pigeons, and dragonflies were arriving at Morningstar Castle in siege numbers. Messages from every kingdom and every corner of the magical realms were still flooding in. Many were inquiring about the great magnitude of power that had erupted from Ursula's death and whether it had been taken care of. Some of the messages were simply offers of condolences for Ursula's passing. Nanny had time for none of those. She would reply when she had dealt with Maleficent. But one message would not wait. It was from her sister, informing her that a group of fairies was on its way to help her handle "the odd sisters situation." That was the last thing Nanny needed: a bunch of fairies descending upon Morningstar while Maleficent was there!

Why in Hades does the world choose to fall apart all at once? Leave it to my sister and her silly wish-granting fairies to meddle in things that do not concern them!

Nanny wondered if it was all a ruse to confront Maleficent. She found it difficult to believe the Fairy Godmother cared about the odd sisters. No, she was just being paranoid. How would the fairies even know that Maleficent was on her way to Morningstar? The fairies were coming to discuss the odd sisters. Miss High and Mighty Bibbidi-Bobbidi-Boo was coming to cast judgment on the odd sisters. Simple. Straightforward. Nothing to worry about.

Nanny's gut instincts nagged at her. *No. This convergence will be disastrous.* She was sure of it.

Nanny felt overwhelmed, not only by everything that was happening, but also by the rapid-fire recollections that continued to flash through her mind. It was strange. Her memories were flooding back, but Nanny couldn't remember how she'd *lost* them in the first place.

"You probably put a spell on yourself to forget. Seems like something you would do," Circe said from the doorway, interrupting Nanny's thoughts. Circe was probably right. It was highly likely that Nanny had caused herself to lose her own memories as a way to deal with the pain of her failure to protect Maleficent. It was horrible enough to remember all her own regrets, but to remember Maleficent's memories in such vivid detail was breaking her heart. It was no wonder she had chosen to forget.

Nanny switched the subject, trying to avoid the memories just for a moment. "How are your sisters? Any change?"

Circe shook her head. "No."

Nanny looked sad, lost in her thoughts. She didn't say so, but Circe could tell she was also dreadfully concerned about the odd sisters, and she was worried about Maleficent.

"I don't want you to worry," Circe said finally.

"I know we will find something to wake my sisters. And as for Maleficent, you have Pflanze. You have Tulip. And of course, you have me. We're here. There's nothing Maleficent can do to you with us beside you."

"I'm more worried about my sister and her goody-goody friends, honestly," Nanny said, handing Circe the Fairy Godmother's message. "They're also on their way."

Circe narrowed her eyes. "That is a problem. Is there no way to turn them away? To tell them that they're not wanted?"

Nanny shook her head. "My sister never imagines a situation in which she isn't welcome. Telling her she wasn't wanted wouldn't even register. Turning her away isn't an option. She'll simply look at me blankly and pretend not to understand what I'm saying."

Circe sighed. "Why is she coming? You don't think she's the one who put my sisters to sleep, do you?"

"I honestly don't know. I assumed they were

sleeping because it took so much of their strength to fight the spell they created to help Ursula," Nanny explained. "But they still won't wake. Nothing I've tried has helped. Nothing you've done has worked. And now I'm wondering if the fairies *have* somehow intervened."

Circe's eyes flashed with anger. "Intervened how? If they've hurt them . . ."

"No, their magic doesn't allow them to hurt anyone, not even their enemies," Nanny said. "And your sisters have never been their enemies, not really. Yes, they've sided with Maleficent in the past. The odd sisters have helped her before, but they never hounded the fairies. It seems my sister's been stepping out of her providence lately. She's taking her role of Fairy Godmother too far. Princess Aurora is not her charge, but if she has taken it upon herself to cast an endless sleep on your sisters, I'd wager it's for the protection of her beloved princesses."

Circe frowned. "I thought Cinderella was her only princess."

"She is, and is living happily. But I suspect my sister may be growing weary with not much to do. So she's putting her round little nose in where it doesn't belong." Nanny sighed. "Enough about my sister, I just hope she doesn't bring those insufferable little sycophants, the three good fairies, with her."

"You have no love for fairies, do you, Nanny?" Circe asked with a smile. "I don't blame you. If it's any consolation, I don't see you as a fairy. In my heart, you are a witch and always have been."

"Thank you, dear. Your sisters once said something quite similar to both me and Maleficent. Something about being born a fairy but having a witch's heart. I suppose they were right."

Circe considered that. "Well, if you think about it, a fairy can just as easily be a witch, as a human might, if she's capable of the right sort of magic. But with you, there's a little more to it, I think. It's what I see in your heart. You don't share fairy sensibilities."

"Too right! And I thank you, my dear, but—"

Nanny was interrupted by a loud knock on the front door of the castle that made them both jump. Nanny's heart sank. She wasn't ready to face Maleficent just yet.

Circe took Nanny's hand and squeezed it, reminding Nanny she was there to protect her. How Nanny wished she had always had Circe in her life. What would it have been like always to have had such a young powerful witch willing to do good by her side? A witch who had an open heart and none of the bigotry that ran so deep in the fairy community? Nanny had been preparing herself for Maleficent's rage, but she wasn't quite ready to meet it. She wasn't ready for the condemnation. Maybe when Maleficent saw Circe, she would see into her heart and see Nanny through Circe's eyes. And maybe she would hold less judgment in her own heart for Nanny by virtue of the love Circe held for her—an old woman who only now had remembered who she really was.

Hudson came into the room with a grave look

on his face. He was pale and seemed very uncomfortable.

"What is it, Hudson? What's the matter? Who is here?" Nanny asked.

"It's Queen Snow White, ma'am. She's sent a message."

For the love of all things good, what could Snow possibly want with us? Nanny wondered.

Hudson shifted his weight back and forth awkwardly. "And the page, ma'am, he says the message is from Queen Snow White *and* her mother."

It wasn't like Hudson to ask questions, especially about royalty, but he couldn't stop himself. "Ma'am, has Queen Snow White lost her senses? Everyone knows the legend of the old queen's demise. Please excuse my impertinence, but . . ."

"My dear Hudson, please don't concern yourself with this. I assure you, Queen Snow White hasn't lost her senses," Nanny said firmly.

"Yes, ma'am," Hudson said nervously. He didn't look at all comfortable with the knowledge that the infamous queen Grimhilde somehow still inhabited this world.

"The old queen's disposition has changed since her death, Hudson. Please don't worry," Nanny said. Hudson gave Nanny a look she had grown accustomed to—a look of pure awe, because she had read his thoughts.

"I'll take that message now, Hudson, if you don't mind," Nanny said with a coy smile.

Hudson fumbled for the message and placed it in Nanny's outstretched hand. "Of course. I-I'm sorry!" he stammered.

"Please, Hudson, don't worry. Why don't you go downstairs for a nice cup of tea? I think it will do you some good."

"Poor Hudson," Circe said with a laugh as the witches watched him walk away. "What does the letter say?"

"Let me see," Nanny said. Circe looked on, analyzing the expression on Nanny's face rather than reading her thoughts. Clearly the queens weren't sending good news.

"It seems your sisters left a book at the old queen's castle during one of their visits when Snow was still a small girl," Nanny explained. "A book of fairy tales. Apparently, the old queen used to read this book to Snow when she was little, and there was a story about a Dragon Witch who puts a young woman to sleep for her own protection. They're wondering now, with everything going on with Aurora and Maleficent, if this book foretold their story."

Circe didn't know what to make of that, but Nanny continued before she could question it. "The part that is most concerning to them is that this book seems to be predicting everyone's stories. Not just Aurora's, but Snow's, Ariel's, Tulip's, Cinderella's, even yours! The old queen and Snow White are worried the book is spellbound."

Circe didn't even want to think about what it would mean if her sisters had spellbound the book. "Do you think it is?"

"Spellbound? No, I think I know this book. I think it is simply a recording of time. It's not prophecy or spell-work. I don't think even your sisters would do such a thing."

Circe wasn't as sure. "If my sisters did spellbind that book, you know Queen Grimhilde will want revenge. Everyone will."

Nanny shuddered at the notion. If the odd sisters *had* spellbound the book, not even Circe would be able to protect them from the repercussions of their grievous misdeeds.

"We need to see this book. Circe, can you write to Snow White and ask her to send it? The only way to know if the book is spellbound is for you to look at it. If your sisters have done this—"

Circe cut her off. "It would be devastating."

Nanny felt a terrible chill as she thought about the destruction the odd sisters had caused over the years. She felt a tugging in her heart that she hadn't felt in longer than she'd like to recollect. She wondered if they should even bring the odd sisters back. She had promised to help Circe wake them simply because that was what Circe wished, and Nanny wanted nothing more than to make Circe happy. But would that really be the best thing for Circe? Would Circe ever truly be happy with her sisters in the world, inflicting death and destruction on everything they touched? Circe would spend the rest of her long life righting her sisters' wrongs and helping those her sisters hurt. Would she ever reach her full potential in their shadows? Nanny was heartbroken in the wake of that revelation. *I can't refuse to help her now. I can't go back on my word. Even if it would be the best thing for Circe if her sisters stayed asleep.*

Circe's face filled with grief. She had heard Nanny's thoughts and felt betrayed by them. "How could you?" Circe cried as all the color drained from Nanny's face.

Nanny hadn't meant for Circe to hear what she was thinking. "I want only to protect you, Circe. I promise you," she insisted.

Circe stood silently, not knowing what to say. She felt numb and close to tears. She couldn't look

Nanny in the eye. "I think I will go home, write to Snow White, and ask her more about this book," Circe said. "Besides, I think I could use a change of scenery."

CHAPTER XV

THE WITCHES
IN THE MIRRORS

In the time Aurora had been in the dream realm, she had never been able to speak with anyone who appeared in the mirrored chamber; she was always just an observer. And now that she was speaking with someone in this lonely, dreary place, it had to be with these women, these *witches*, these bizarre raving lunatics she could hardly understand.

"Oh, that isn't nice, Princess. Not nice at all."

"Yes, watch your manners, dear!"

"Didn't your stupid fairy godmothers teach you manners?"

Aurora didn't know what to say. She still wasn't entirely convinced that the witches were actually speaking to her. She remembered one night when she was watching her cousin Tulip. She could have sworn that Tulip was talking directly to her, but it turned out she was talking to her cat, Pflanze. Aurora had felt silly for answering Tulip, and she'd promised herself she wouldn't make that mistake again.

"Oh, we're talking to you, Princess! Oh, yes, we are!"

Aurora narrowed her eyes at the witches in the mirror.

"Oh, yes, Aurora! We see you!" The two witches in the left and right mirrors were waving manically, eyes bulging as they smiled at her like madwomen.

Even though they all looked exactly alike, the witch in the middle somehow seemed older than the other two. She wasn't joining in their antics. She just stood there, staring right at Aurora, taking her measure. "So you're the princess Aurora. Maleficent will be so pleased that we found you."

"Who . . . who are you? And how do you know Maleficent?" Aurora said hesitantly.

"My name is Lucinda, and these two rather animated witches are my sisters, Ruby and Martha. As for Maleficent, well . . . she is a very old friend of ours," the witch in the middle replied.

Aurora studied the odd sisters. The women were clearly magical, but Aurora sensed that their powers were limited by the twilight magic of the dreamscape.

"Are you Circe's sisters?" the princess asked, putting it together. She had seen a beautiful young witch named Circe at Morningstar Castle with her cousin Princess Tulip. Circe had been fretting over her sisters, who were trapped in the land of dreams.

"How does the sleeping Rose know our little sister?" Ruby screamed, her face contorting itself horribly.

Lucinda shot her sister an evil glare, silencing her. "Don't squawk, Ruby. And let's please try to talk plainly and in a straight line for the princess here. This place is confusing enough without us adding to the bedlam."

"Oh, no! Are we doing that again, Lucinda? Please! Please tell us we don't have to!" Ruby and Martha yelled.

"Tell us how you know our sister!" Ruby snarled, making Aurora jump back in fright.

"Stop this, Ruby, and let the girl answer the question!" Lucinda scolded her.

Clearly Lucinda is in charge of the other two, the princess thought.

"She's not in charge!" squeaked Martha, reading Aurora's mind.

"Oh, you know she's in charge! She always has been!" said Ruby.

"Sisters, please! Let the girl speak. She was going to tell us about our sister," Lucinda said.

"Well, I wasn't, actually. It seems to me since I have information you want, it might be better to keep it to myself," Aurora said bravely.

Lucinda smirked slyly. "I see."

What happened next was entirely unexpected.

Lucinda stepped through the mirror like a specter from the fathoms of death, her long bony hands grasping at the princess. Terrified, Aurora fell backward onto the ground, suddenly seized by a terrible burning sensation within her.

The three sisters cackled. "Careful, dear! You haven't discovered *all* the magic in this place, or the magic within your own soul. Now tell us what you know about our little sister!"

CHAPTER XVI

THE ODD SISTERS' GRIMOIRES

Circe sat on the floor of her eerily quiet house, surrounded by her sisters' books. She had written her letter to Snow and was now searching for something—anything—that could help her wake her sisters. The house's stained glass windows, depicting her sisters' many adventures, did nothing to inspire ideas about how to wake them up. It was so strange being in that house alone, flipping through her sisters' books and going through their pantry. She had found countless sleeping enchantments and their antidotes, but nothing to bring someone out of the realm of dreams—if that was in fact where her sisters were. If history told Circe anything, it was that there had to be some addendum to whatever curse had sent her sisters to the land of dreams in the first place. It was likely that the person who had cursed them would have to be the one to bring them back. Nevertheless, she searched.

The black onyx crows that flanked the fireplace stared into nothingness while Circe searched in vain through her sisters' many spell books and journals. Circe had to use all her willpower not to be distracted by the stories inside. Her sisters were so much older than her. She'd often wondered what their lives were like before they had to care for her. They never spoke of it—of the time before she was in their world, or of their parents, or how they had died. Circe's childhood was a mystery to her. She remembered nothing of her upbringing. Whenever she had tried to ask her sisters about that time, they had simply rambled off senseless words so that she would drop the subject. If only her power to rewind and look at time worked on her. She couldn't help wondering if those years were documented somewhere in the books. When she was a child, her sisters' spell books would either refuse to open or scream in pain if she touched them. Her sisters had been alerted anytime she had tried to spy on them. But now her sisters weren't there. She needed only to open the books, which simultaneously thrilled and frightened her. If her sisters' protection spells were broken, did that mean they would never recover from their ordeal? Usually a spell stopped working only when a witch was dead.

Circe recalled Nanny telling her how Circe's spell had gone haywire when Ursula had taken Circe's soul. Nanny had worried that something terrible had happened to Circe, but she had recovered, hadn't she? That at least gave Circe hope.

As Circe sat with a stack of books before her, the light coming through a stained glass window featuring a single red apple caught her eye. She had seen the window countless times over the years, and she knew the meaning behind it. She knew fragments of the story, anyway, as she knew only bits of the tales that had inspired all the windows in her home. But right then, the apple caught her eye and tugged at her heart. She thought of Snow White's book and wondered what secrets it might hold.

Just then, she heard a light tapping on the doorbell, so soft that she almost missed it. She opened the door to find a tiny owl hitting its beak against the large brass bell visitors normally rang to make their presence known. The tiny creature was so enchanted by his own reflection in the brass that he was completely oblivious to Circe.

"Come in, little one. I will give you a biscuit," Circe said, scooping him up. The little gray owl hooted his thanks as Circe placed him gently on the kitchen table. He promptly stuck out his tiny foot, waiting for Circe to take the scroll that had been tethered there. He looked somewhat wobbly as he stood on one foot. Circe had to wonder how long the little owl had been delivering messages and with what success. She found the biscuit tin, broke a biscuit in half, and gave it to the owl to nibble on while she read the message. He gave her a strange look, as if she was being stingy.

"You're a wee one, little sir. You may have the

other half when you've finished that," Circe said as she unraveled the scroll and began to read.

Dear Circe,

Thank you for your lovely heartfelt letter. I wanted you to know I received it and my mother has agreed to help me with the instructions for the travel charm you sent. There is so much more I want to say to you, but since we will be together soon, I think I will leave it until then.

With kindest regards,
Queen Snow White

Circe was ecstatic at the idea of finally meeting her cousin Queen Snow White. She looked down at her dress and laughed. *Well, I'd better change my clothes!* Circe was completely disheveled from the events that had befallen her in the past weeks. She hadn't even bothered to look in a mirror—and she didn't dare now for fear of how frightful she surely looked.

The owl tapped his little foot on the wooden table, waiting for his reward. She tossed him the other half of the biscuit while she scribbled a hurried note to Nanny, letting her know Snow was on her way to Morningstar.

Once she cleaned herself up and heard what Queen Snow White had to say, she would continue searching through her sisters' books. Circe just hoped she could find something before it was too late.

CHAPTER XVII

THE TREE LORDS

Pflanze was sitting quietly in the solarium with the odd sisters. She was keeping herself occupied by looking at the solstice tree, its silver and gold ornaments glittering by the candlelight, when a dreadful feeling came over her. She sat very still. Her ears perked up as she felt a terrible tremor. Something large was approaching Morningstar Castle. As it drew closer, the decorations on the tree started to shake violently, falling from the branches and shattering into splinters all around Pflanze. She bolted away from the tree and let out a loud screech to get someone's attention. She rarely used her voice, and it sounded strange to her. She decided to call Nanny telepathically, but before she could, the solarium doors burst open, revealing a worried-looking Nanny and Tulip.

What is it? What's happening? Pflanze asked, looking more frightened than Nanny had ever seen her.

"We don't know! We thought the odd sisters had woken up and that's why you were howling!" Nanny cried. She looked around the room, frantically trying to find the cause of the shaking. The room grew dim, and then everything went black.

"Stop!" Nanny raised her hands skyward, creating a brilliant silver light. In its glow, they could see the source of the vibrations. Massive trees had surrounded the solarium. Trees larger than any others, trees thought to have been extinct. Trees that had ruled the kingdom in the time before men or women.

Nanny knew at once why they were there.

Tulip looked up at the trees in shock. She had dreamed of the creatures as she'd read their history, but she'd never thought that she would ever see them in real life.

"They won't hurt us. That's not their way!" Tulip screamed. She was afraid Nanny would harm them with her magic.

Before Nanny could answer, there came a rapid knock from the front door of the castle. Nanny and Pflanze turned their attention in that direction as Tulip dashed out of the room to see who was there. When Hudson opened the door, Prince Popinjay ran into the castle, looking rather pleased with himself. "Tulip! The Tree Lords! They're here!"

Tulip laughed. "Yes, my love, I know. But what are *you* doing here?" She brushed the leaves and twigs from his velvet jacket, straightening the ribbons at his sleeves.

"I had to follow them when I saw they were headed to the castle, my love! But they assured me they mean you no harm. Their leader, Oberon, he wants to speak with you," Popinjay said.

Tulip blinked a few times. She was dumbfounded. "With me? But why?"

"I don't know, my darling. You'd best ask them yourself."

"I suppose I'd better go out and meet him, then," Tulip said.

"Now, darling, I know you don't fear Oberon, but please be wary," Nanny said. "Don't agree to anything. Don't make promises that are not within your power to keep. And whatever you do, please warn them that Maleficent is on her way and will not hesitate to use fire to protect herself."

Tulip nodded, taking in everything Nanny was saying with grave importance. "Of course."

"Choose your words wisely, my dear. As you've read, the Tree Lords speak very straightforwardly. There is never room for interpretation, and you should use similar language. Always speak as directly as possible. Your words matter now more than ever. Misinterpretation could be disastrous. Now go! Speak to the King of the Fairies!"

Chapter XVIII

Oberon, King of the Fairies

Princess Tulip Morningstar stood in the shadow of Oberon. She couldn't have fathomed how tall the Tree Lords were without seeing them with her own eyes. Her imagination was great—but seeing the sheer awesomeness of Oberon and his army in reality was more earth-shattering than anything she could have conjured in her wildest of dreams. He stood taller than the Lighthouse of the Gods, dwarfing Tulip, who felt smaller than she ever had before. Despite this, somehow she was not afraid.

She stood silently, waiting for Oberon to speak first. Technically, he was visiting her lands, but he had ruled there first, long before the time of men and women. Princess Tulip wanted to show him the respect he deserved. Luckily, she didn't have to wait long. Oberon's voice rumbled from overhead, shaking his branches. His leaves cascaded around Tulip as his sonorous voice—one befitting a venerable and powerful being—boomed out of the darkness.

"Princess Tulip, I am honored to meet you. Would you mind if I took you within my branches so we may speak face to face?"

"Not at all, I would like that," Tulip replied. And she meant it. She had never felt so fearless. As Oberon's branches gingerly grabbed her, she didn't fear that she would be crushed within his powerful clutches. He placed her safely atop the balcony of the Lighthouse of the Gods, where they could meet almost face to face.

"Ah, there you are. You have the face of a queen. You possess beauty that surpasses my imaginings."

Tulip smiled at the Tree Lord, examining the lines in his face. His features were defined by his bark and the deep cracks in his trunk. And it seemed to Tulip that he might have the most benevolent face she had ever beheld.

"Kind words, my dear," Oberon said, reading her mind. "We are here to protect you from the Dark Fairy, Maleficent. Long ago, she destroyed the Fairylands. We left it to the other creatures of the forest to exact revenge while we slumbered. But now that we have awoken, we cannot let her come to our lands—your lands—and destroy those you love, dear Tulip."

The princess didn't understand why Oberon felt such a devotion to her. She didn't know what she had done to deserve such an honor.

"We were slumbering in darkness and obscurity for what felt like a millennium, until your interest woke us," Oberon answered. "Your stories, your imaginings of us brought me and my brethren out of our slumber and gave us life once again. We were forgotten in these lands after we were driven off by the Cyclopean Giants following the Great War. But your thirst for knowledge has sparked life back into us, and for that we are grateful. Without your interest and devotion, we would not exist. I witnessed many things while I slept, my dear. There are many wrongs in this world that we intend to right. It is time to take my place among the fairies once more as their benefactor. To deserve that place again, I must destroy the Dark Fairy known as Maleficent for her crimes against the Fairylands."

"If you don't mind my asking, why punish Maleficent now for burning the Fairylands so many years ago?" Tulip said.

Oberon seemed to be contemplating Tulip's question. "Because, my dear, we were sleeping before. We watched her atrocities while we slumbered. We watched in horror as she destroyed every living creature in those lands—all except the fairies themselves. It took the fairies years to repair the damage. Never once did she return to see if anyone had survived. She didn't even care to find out whether her adopted mother still lived. We were helpless, as if trapped in a nightmare, seeing all of this without being able to do anything about it. But now that we've awoken, there is no choice but to avenge nature by making Maleficent pay for what she's done. She is a danger to all living things. She is a danger to herself. She is a danger to those you love!"

Tulip was speechless. She knew nothing of Maleficent other than the fact that she had put Tulip's cousin to sleep on her sixteenth birthday. Tulip could not defend the Dark Fairy. "May I ask another question?"

The Tree Lord laughed. "You may ask anything you wish, little one. If it weren't for you, we would not be here."

Tulip smiled. "Thank you. Who put you to sleep? I know you ruled these lands long before men and women came to the shores. And I know you and your kind left after the Great War between your kindred and the Cyclopean Giants. But where did you go? Was it the Fairylands?"

Oberon's laugh rumbled from his chest. "Indeed it was the Fairylands, my dear. We had decided to wander until we could find a place to call home when we came across the fairies. They were living in fear, under constant threat of ogre attacks. The vile beasts had swarmed the Fairylands, burning them again and again. They'd killed everything and everyone in their path. So we stayed, fought off the ogres, and made the Fairylands our home until we wandered into obscurity for our rest."

"You put yourselves to sleep, then?" Tulip asked.

"I did, my sweet. Our kind live many lifetimes, like your nanny, but infinitely more. Without sleeping for a number of years, we would wither and die. Of course, we take the risk of being forgotten if we cease to exist in the imaginations of the various prevailing inhabitants of the lands. But someone always brings us out of our slumber, like you did, my little one."

"My nanny, the one you know as—"

"Yes, the One of Legends. She's one of the most powerful beings of the Fairylands," Oberon interrupted.

Tulip looked surprised. She had just gotten used to the idea of her nanny being a witch, and now Oberon was telling her she was a fairy.

"Yes, my dear, she is a fairy of the highest rank. Should she want to admit it or not, she is of that realm and always shall be," Oberon said, reading Tulip's thoughts. "She is the purest of fairy kind. I ceased to sense her magic in the world as I slept. I thought she was gone from us forever, but lately I have sensed her once again. Did you awaken her the way you woke me, my little one?"

Tulip shook her head. "No, it was Pflanze, the odd sisters' cat. Or so Nanny believes, anyway."

Oberon's laugh echoed through his branches, shaking his leaves and making them cascade around Tulip once again. "The odd sisters! They are still in this world? I stopped feeling their spirits after Ursula died. I feared they were lost to us, leaving us with the best parts of themselves." Oberon smiled at the confused expression on Tulip's face. "Oh, yes, I know the odd sisters. All their deeds, all their secrets, all their betrayals and loves—but they are not for me to speak of. What concerns me now is making the Dark Fairy pay for her transgressions. I have felt her coming here and her dark intentions. It was torture for me to hear the screams of our brethren when Maleficent burned the Fairylands. They burned, and I was powerless to do anything about it. But now we are free. And we have been waiting a very long time to make the Dark Fairy pay with her life."

From far away, Tulip heard a tiny scream. Oberon heard it, too. He looked down to see Nanny standing at the base of the lighthouse.

"Come up here, my dear, use your wings," Oberon commanded. A moment later, Nanny appeared beside Tulip and hovered in the air.

"Only for you, Oberon," Nanny replied.

The King of the Fairies looked tenderly at Nanny. "And I suppose you're going to try to make a case for your former charge, your daughter? You're going to try to save her from my wrath, even though she deserves it? It breaks my heart to hurt you, my wee one, it really does, but I cannot let her deeds go unpunished. And how did she repay you for your kindness to her? She nearly killed everyone in the Fairylands. She nearly killed you, and she still may."

"You know it was a mistake," Nanny insisted. "You know it was my fault. If you have to hold someone accountable, punish me."

Oberon chuckled. "You have punished yourself far too much already, my dear one. There is nothing I can do to you that you have not already done to yourself."

Nanny was heartbroken. "But so has Maleficent. The odd sisters told me she punished herself for years. She tortured herself for what she did!"

Oberon shook his head. "She's learned nothing from it. She's only slipped further into darkness. Her deeds are not redemptive. Had she taken another path, had she become the witch you hoped she would be, we wouldn't be here. You know that I speak the truth. And you know that I am compassionate and fair. I don't dole out punishment unjustly. Use your powers. See her crimes. I saw them all as they happened. You refused. That's probably your only crime against her."

"What of my sister's part in all of this?" Nanny asked. "What of the three good fairies? Are they to flitter off into the sunset as usual without even—"

Oberon interrupted her. "No, my dear, they will not. But I will not deal with the good fairies until their charge is safe and her kingdom is no longer asleep. As for your sister, she is one of the reasons I am here. She has disappointed me greatly over the years. I intend to restore compassion and open-mindedness to the Fairylands once again. For far too long have I seen a corruption of fairy magic, and in my name! This will not stand!" Oberon was becoming angry, his voice causing the earth to shake.

"Excuse me, King Oberon?" Tulip said softly.

The King of the Fairies looked down at Tulip, remembering she was there. "Yes, dear heart?"

"Your voice, it is so loud, I'm afraid you will shatter Mr. Fresnel's lens, which helps light the way of the many ships that traverse our kingdom," she said, motioning to the beacon in the lighthouse.

Oberon laughed. "Yes, my dear, you are right.

And he was rather crafty. He was never drawn to the mines like other dwarfs. He always preferred the light. He worked very closely with my enemy Vitruvius, the Cyclopean King, to create the most magnificent lighthouse of any age. I see your castle is built around that lighthouse. But I will not hold that against him or you. He was a true artist and craftsman, an absolute gentleman, and quite articulate for a dwarf. But I digress."

Oberon stopped and looked down at the strange expression on Nanny's face. "Am I boring you with my stories again, my dear one?"

"No. I was just thinking. I should cast a cloaking spell around you and the other Tree Lords. I don't want Maleficent to know you're here when she arrives," she said firmly.

Oberon's face became grave. "I see."

"Please give her a chance," Nanny said. "Please don't hurt her."

"I promise to give you the opportunity to speak with her and to let her know how much you still love her. If she loves you in return, I will show her compassion. I may even spare her life," Oberon agreed.

"Will you give her a chance to redeem herself?"

"I will, my wee fairy, you have my word. But I'm afraid she will disappoint you once again."

CHAPTER XIX

DAUGHTER OF
DESPAIR

Nanny and Tulip returned to the castle and gathered with Popinjay in the morning room. Nanny looked sick with worry, and it made Tulip's heart hurt to see her in such a state. Tulip wanted to take Nanny in her arms and cover her face with kisses, but she was afraid if she did, it would make Nanny cry. "Please don't worry, Nanny. Oberon promised to give Maleficent a chance. I don't think he will hurt her."

Nanny didn't answer; she just stared off into nothingness, lost in her own thoughts.

"Nanny, are you okay? Here, let me ring for some tea." As Tulip went to pull the bell, an explosion of green light burst from the fireplace. Tulip was sent flying across the room and landed at Nanny's feet. The room was overwhelmed with green light and flames. As Popinjay helped Tulip to her feet, Maleficent walked out of the hearth and stood before them, tall and imposing, with green flames lingering around her like an evil aura.

"Maleficent!" cried Nanny.

"Well, isn't this quaint? A little gathering, smaller but much more distinguished than I would have imagined. I'm sorry I missed the ceremony for the *great* sea queen, but I did see it through the eyes of my crows. It was very . . . *touching*," Maleficent sneered.

Her voice was unmistakable to Nanny. Older, yes, but it was still her daughter's voice. Maleficent was beautiful, as always. Her long black robes, accented in purple, and her sharp features fit her formidable personality. There was a confidence in Maleficent that Nanny hadn't seen when her charge was younger, and the grown fairy emanated an air of power and majesty. She was probably the most striking woman Nanny had ever beheld. *But her horns! Her beautiful horns are covered in back wrappings. . . .*

"Maleficent," Nanny said again. It seemed to Tulip that Nanny was diminished and heartbroken. She looked pale and dwarfed in comparison to the fierce firestorm of a fairy.

"Welcome to my court, Maleficent," Tulip said, trying to give Nanny a minute to compose herself.

"Tulip, is it? Yes, that's right. Tulip. I'm sorry to hear about your mother. Although I can't take credit for her sleeping spell. That was the good fairies' doing." Maleficent looked at Tulip for some time, taking her measure, soaking in her beauty. "I always found it astounding how remarkably alike you and Aurora look, considering—"

"Maleficent, why are you here?" Nanny asked, finding her voice after hearing Maleficent speak to Tulip so flippantly.

"Why, to say good-bye to the great sea witch, of course. To show her the respect she *deserved*." Maleficent smirked.

"You never loved Ursula. Why are you truly here, Maleficent?" Nanny asked.

"You can thank the good fairies for my visit," Maleficent replied. "I wouldn't have come at all had they not interfered with my curse. But now that they have, now that there is a chance the sleeping princess will wake, I do need help. Don't you see? Prince Phillip is in love with the girl. I cannot have him waking her. You'd think the fairies would have thought of something more creative. Practically every princess in peril has been saved by Love's First Kiss! For goodness' sake, between witches and fairies, can't we think of something more original? I'm weary of this. Why must a young girl need a man to save her? Why can't a princess fight for her own life, break her own curse? Why must it always be a prince? By Hades, I want to kill Prince Phillip on principle, just so we don't have yet one more prince kissing some helpless sleeping girl, making her feel like she has to marry him out of gratitude."

Popinjay cleared his throat. "I wouldn't expect

Tulip to marry me just because I saved her—not that she needs saving by me or anyone else."

"Well, aren't you a modern man of the age?" Maleficent taunted the young prince. "But if I recall, it was Ursula and Circe who saved Tulip, not you."

"She saved herself," Popinjay said. He puffed out his chest to try to make himself seem larger and more imposing.

Maleficent laughed. "If by 'saving herself' you mean jumping off a cliff in an attempt to take her own life because she was heartbroken, only to be saved by witches, then you are correct. Though I will say her story is more original than most. I will give her that."

Tulip hated hearing Maleficent speak to Popinjay that way. She wondered if the Dark Fairy had even noticed the Tree Lords standing outside the morning room. She felt pride, knowing they were there to protect her from the horrible fairy. Tulip tried to imagine the Dark Fairy standing before her as a little girl, helpless and afraid, but she couldn't. This woman seemed to be afraid of nothing. Her confidence was astounding. She truly didn't seem to have one ounce of fear in her heart.

"Why are you really here, Maleficent?" Nanny asked again.

"The odd sisters were supposed to help me with something very important. As addled and scatterbrained as they were, they were the only people left in this realm I could trust. Now I am forced to ask the very person I trust least for help," Maleficent replied.

"You must have known the odd sisters were asleep! But still you came, and you didn't even know who would be here to greet you!" Nanny said.

"I sensed great power—yours and another's. A powerful witch who no longer seems to be in your company."

"You mean Circe."

Maleficent paused to consider that for a moment. "Ah, Circe. I should have known it would be the odd sisters' little sister. Of course. It all makes sense. I had to come on the slim chance you two could help me. I can't break the addendum to the curse alone. I need three witches to break this fairy magic. Don't you see? Even if I do away with Prince Phillip, there's still a chance some other young man might wake her from her slumber. We have to keep Aurora in the dreamscape. We must never let her wake!"

"There is no way you will get Circe to agree to help you," Nanny pointed out. "She is not like her sisters. She's not going to harm a child simply because you want her to, and neither will I!"

Maleficent sighed. "What will it take for you and Circe to help me unbind the good fairies' spell? Must I prostrate myself in some fashion so you will find my cause worthy?"

"I will not answer for Circe, Maleficent," Nanny protested. "She knows only some of your story. She must know everything, as must I, before we can even consider helping you."

"Where shall I begin?" Maleficent asked.

Nanny took her enchanted hand mirror from her pocket, more thankful than ever that the odd sisters had given it to her many years ago.

"Show me Circe!" she commanded.

Circe's stern face appeared in the glass. "What is it, Nanny? Is everything okay?"

"Circe, Maleficent is here, and she would like to share her story with us. She thinks if she does, we will be willing to help her unbind the good fairies' spell."

"She can share her story, but I will not harm that child!" Circe replied.

"I do not want to harm her. I want to protect her," insisted Maleficent.

"Then share your story, Maleficent. I'm eager to hear what you have to say," Circe said.

"I think Nanny can tell this part best," said Maleficent, surprising Nanny by using her name for the first time since she had arrived.

Nanny sighed. She could no longer put off remembering her daughter's heartbreaking memories. "Tulip, dear, can you please ring Violet for that tea? This is going to take some time."

157

CHAPTER XX

THE DARK FAIRY'S BIRTHDAY

The morning of the fairy exams, Maleficent woke to find that Diablo still hadn't come home. He wasn't on his perch waiting for her, like she had hoped. She tried to banish all the negative thoughts plaguing her mind. She needed to focus on her exam, but she found herself distracted. Maleficent was convinced something horrible had happened to Diablo.

She called for one of her favorite crows. "Opal, my pet, will you go see if you can find Diablo? I'm worried about him." Opal gave a soft caw and flew out the window. Maleficent watched her as she circled over the Fairylands. She knew if anyone could find Diablo, it was Opal. For a brief moment, she could see what Opal saw as she headed toward the thick woodlands. Maleficent had come to realize it was her fondness for Opal that allowed her to see though her eyes. She still needed practice to see clearly through her pets' eyes, though, rather than experiencing the flashing images she was seeing now. She looked around, yawning. She felt a little better knowing Opal was out looking for Diablo. And she loved waking up in her tree house. The view of the Fairylands was beautiful from up there, and she wondered what it would be like to live life from that vantage point. Perhaps one day she would know.

"Maleficent! Come down and have your breakfast. You're going to be late for the exam!" Nanny said from the doorway, startling the girl.

"How long have you been standing there?" Maleficent asked.

Nanny gave her a sad smile. "Long enough to know Diablo hasn't come home. Not to worry, my sweet. He is safe. I can feel him in the world. I'm sure Opal will find him. Trust me."

Maleficent and Nanny went down to the kitchen. Nanny had been up all night, baking various pastries, which she had arranged beautifully on pretty flower-patterned plates.

"Are we having guests for breakfast as well?" Maleficent asked.

Nanny looked up from the pot of tea she was making. "What? No! Why do you ask that?"

"You've baked so much!" Maleficent's yellow eyes were wide but happy. Her long black hair was wild, as it often was when she first woke, and Nanny thought her horns were beautiful. They seemed to have finally stopped growing less than a year earlier and were a lovely deep shade of gray, which complemented her yellow eyes. And Nanny had noticed Maleficent's skin was a very light shade of lavender. That meant she was either happy or worried. Maybe both. Nanny had realized years before that her daughter's skin tone changed depending on her mood. At least today she wasn't green, which would have indicated she was either angry or extremely sad. Green was a color Nanny hadn't seen on Maleficent in quite a while. Nanny blinked a few times, taking in her daughter's beauty, before she realized Maleficent was waiting for a reply.

"Oh, yes, you know I bake when I'm nervous. Now eat something before you have to get ready for your exam."

Nanny was definitely more nervous than Maleficent. Not only was the table filled with artfully decorated pastries and little cakes, but she had also made an assortment of preserves and clotted creams and a lovely lemon curd. Those sat beside bowls filled with fresh fruit. "Does nothing on the table look good? Would you like me to make you some porridge?"

"No, Nanny, I'm fine. Everything looks beautiful. Sit down and have some breakfast with me." Maleficent gestured to the chair next to her.

Nanny shook her head. "I can't, my dear! No time! Now eat!"

Maleficent grabbed a large chocolate chip scone, broke off a piece, and covered it with clotted cream.

"Try the cinnamon berry preserves, my dear,

161

and the maple butter. I made those just for you," Nanny insisted. Maleficent had intended to try them; the maple butter was her favorite. "I thought you would like that, my dear. Now hurry up and finish! You'd better go get ready soon."

Nanny stopped fussing for a minute and looked at her daughter. "My dear one! I almost forgot! Open that package on the table. It's a gift for your birthday."

Maleficent smiled as she tore open the brown paper. Inside the parcel was a set of beautiful black robes edged in silver and embroidered with silver ravens and crows. She had never seen anything more beautiful. "Thank you, Nanny!" Maleficent flew into her mother's arms and kissed her on the cheek.

"My darling, do you know how beautiful you are?" Nanny asked. Maleficent's pale cheeks turned pink, so Nanny changed the subject. "I know you're going to do well today. I just know it. And if you will forgive the suggestion . . . you know I love you just as you are . . . it's just that—"

Maleficent stopped Nanny before she could

continue. "I had already planned to cover my horns."

"Not for me, mind you. Just so there is no reason for my sister to give you grief!"

"I know."

Nanny patted Maleficent on the cheek and then gave her a light kiss. "You know I think your horns are beautiful."

"I know you do." Maleficent flashed her mother a radiant smile, returning the kiss with another. "Thank you, Mother."

CHAPTER XXI

FAIRY EXAMS

Everyone was assembled for the exam in the main garden, which happened to be one of Nanny's favorite places in the Fairylands. The fountain statue was fashioned in the image of Nanny's old friend King Oberon—a large, imposing tree with a kind and wise face. Water cascaded from the statue's full branches, replicating rain. Nanny looked at her daughter with pride as she stood beneath the towering statue, waiting for her exam to start. She looked majestic in her new robes. Maleficent had covered her horns with silver ribbons Nanny had given her, which matched the embroidered silver crows on her gown. Nanny thought Maleficent looked almost grown-up. It made Nanny's heart swell with pride to see what a lovely and intelligent young woman her daughter had become. She'd never imagined Maleficent would want to take the fairy exams. Even if her sister didn't pick Maleficent for wish granting, at least Maleficent was brave enough to take the exams with the other students after everything they had put her through when she was younger.

Merryweather was bossing around Fauna and Flora, as she often did. She was instructing them on the importance of all three passing together as they waited for the exam to start.

"Oh, Maleficent, what are you doing here?" Merryweather said, her nose wrinkled up as if she'd smelled something putrid.

"I'm here to take the exam, of course," Maleficent said, pretending Merryweather and the fairies at her side weren't making ugly faces at her. Maleficent looked around, wondering why the rest of the class was standing off to the side.

Flora followed Maleficent's gaze. "Oh, they aren't taking the exam. They're just here to watch us."

Maleficent frowned. "Why?"

"Because they know they don't have a chance with *us* taking the exams this year," Merryweather said as Flora and Fauna giggled.

Maleficent shook her head. It seemed time had not changed the three. They were the same haughty, arrogant fools they'd always been.

"Even if they're not given wish-granting privileges, surely they will want their certificates for completing the course?" Maleficent said.

"What good is a certificate if you can't perform the most honored of fairy duties?" Flora said, making all three fairies laugh.

Just then, the Fairy Godmother cleared her throat to get everyone's attention. She was standing in front of the fountain to address the group. She wore her customary blue robes and large pink ribbon. Behind her were lovely cherry blossom trees, their petals softly falling around her and the students. "I stand here in the shadow of the Great One, Oberon, King of the Fairies. He was our great benefactor and protector for many years, until he saw fit to drift off into obscurity, leaving my sister and me the burden and privilege of continuing fairy education."

Maleficent scoffed inwardly. Oberon had actually left the honor to Nanny alone, but she had decided to share it with her sister.

"And it is my privilege to once again pick the three students who will venture off into the many kingdoms to spread fairy magic to help their charges, young women and men in need of our special brand of magic. When I was a young fairy, waiting to take my exam, my heart fluttered at the thought of holding a young person's dreams in my hands. It is a great responsibility, and an honor that must not be taken lightly. Only the best of us are granted this status, those of us who are truly good, and good of heart."

Maleficent felt a pain in her stomach as the Fairy Godmother said those last words. *Good of heart.*

"Of course, there are other very honorable, important vocations for the fairies who aren't granted status. You will all use what you have learned here from your instructors at this prestigious and venerable academy wherever your path takes you." The Fairy Godmother paused, smiling at all her students.

"And with that, we shall begin our exams. Each of you will be given a young charge who needs your help. He or she will present you with his or her problem, and it will be your job to figure out the best way to help. You must choose the kind of magic best suited to his or her needs. Remember, even though this is only an exercise and the young men and women standing in for your charges are only here for the purposes of the exam, your magic is still binding. So please, do use caution, and whatever you do, please refrain from using harmful magic."

The Fairy Godmother looked right at Maleficent when she said *harmful magic*. She might as well have punctuated the sentence with *Maleficent*.

Nanny and the Fairy Godmother created a series of paths, each spinning out in a different direction. Fauna and Flora grimaced at the idea of having to take their paths alone, without their friend

168

Merryweather to help them. "Fairy Godmother, can't we do the exam together?" Flora asked. "The three of us, Fauna, Merryweather, and I?"

The Fairy Godmother thought about it for a moment. "It's not the custom by any means, but I don't see the harm."

Nanny objected. "If Flora, Fauna, and Merryweather take the exam together, then they should be counted as one fairy. Should they perform highest in the class, their wish-granting status should be granted to them as a group. Therefore, two other fairies should be selected, as well."

"Well, I'm not sure . . ." The Fairy Godmother's voice trailed off. But a demure golden-haired fairy dressed in sparkling blue spoke up.

"I would like to take the exam, then," the fairy said softly.

Maleficent smiled at the fairy in blue. "Then you should! Come stand by me." She looked at the other students who had just been there to watch. "Everyone who wants to take the exams should. Don't let those fools intimidate you."

Slowly, many of the other fairies stepped forward. Merryweather, Fauna, and Flora looked around nervously at the large group that had decided to compete against them. Watching the fairies, Maleficent had to laugh.

"What are you laughing at?" sniped Flora.

"Shhh, Flora, don't speak to that creature! She won't be laughing when she fails the exam," said Fauna.

Maleficent ignored her, but the Blue Fairy shot Fauna a nasty look. "Fauna, leave her alone!" She took Maleficent by the hand and led her away from the trio. "Don't worry about them, Maleficent. They're just nervous you will do better than them. You were always a good student."

Maleficent couldn't stop looking at the Blue Fairy. Her skin was luminescent. Her glow seemed to come from within, as if her goodness was too awesome to be contained. "I wish you would have stayed in school. I hope you know not all of us hated you," the fairy continued.

Maleficent smiled and squeezed the Blue Fairy's

hand as the two watched the Fairy Godmother and Nanny create additional paths for the students to follow. Finally, the Fairy Godmother commenced the exams.

"Choose whichever path speaks to your soul," she advised. "You will only have your wits and magic to guide you. Good luck, my dears! Now begin!"

CHAPTER XXII

THE DARK FAIRY'S REVENGE

Taking a deep breath, Maleficent looked back at Nanny. Nanny flashed Maleficent one of her magnificent smiles and mouthed the words *I love you, Daughter.* With one last wave to her mother, Maleficent turned and walked down the path that felt like it might be hers. She soon found herself in a world that was very unlike the Fairylands.

Maleficent was standing near a small well that lay in the shadow of a beautiful castle with many spires. The castle's roofs resembled red witch hats, and the surrounding lands were lush, green, and heavily wooded. There seemed to be all manner of forest creatures romping about, making the scene more picturesque than if it had been reality. Sitting on the edge of the well and kicking her feet was a young girl with black hair tied with a red ribbon. She was a pretty little thing, with her pale face and apple-red cheeks.

She was crying.

"What's the matter, dear?" Maleficent asked. The girl looked up and gasped. "Shhh, I'm not here to harm you," Maleficent assured her. "What's your name?"

The little girl looked at Maleficent, terrified, but she managed to speak. "My name is Snow White."

"Snow, don't be afraid of me. I'm here to help you. What's the matter, why are you crying?"

"It's my mother. She won't eat or drink, and she spends her days talking to someone who isn't there. She has been ill and heartbroken since my father died . . . and . . ."

"Tell me, please," Maleficent said, coaxing her.

"I'm afraid of her. She's changed since my father died. I'm afraid she may kill me."

"Where is your mother now?" asked Maleficent.

"She spends all her time in her room," Snow replied. "I think she may be going mad. I hear her talking endlessly to someone who isn't there. Sometimes I hear her screaming at something."

Maleficent was concerned. "Has no one looked into this? Is she being tormented by someone or by something? Has anyone been to see her to lift her spirits? To help her through her grief?"

"No one except my father's cousins. But she banished them long ago, along with her best friend, Verona. I'm afraid she is very much alone," Snow replied, wiping tears from her face.

Maleficent didn't understand how the girl could leave her poor grieving mother alone to wither and suffer, but she remained sweet and understanding. "Stay here, my dear. I will see to your mother."

As soon as Maleficent entered the castle, she could feel despair weighing heavily in the air. The home was cursed with sadness and something much worse, something sinister and unnerving. As she made her way up to the queen's chamber, she heard a woman's voice. *How long has this woman been alone up here raving like a madwoman? And to whom is she speaking?* Maleficent whispered a charm that allowed her to see through walls. The effect was much like creating a window. She could see whoever was on the other side, but they were unaware that they were being spied on.

Standing in the middle of the room was a beautiful queen, sobbing with despair as she screamed at a man's image in her mirror. "I command you to tell me the truth!" she shrieked through tears.

A horrible wicked voice came from the man in the mirror. His face was cruel and twisted with hatred. "You killed your mother the day you were born, and your face reminds me of hers."

"That's why you despise me?" The queen was crying so hard she couldn't catch her breath.

"I wish you had died that day, not her!" spat the man in the mirror.

Maleficent was horrified. The man was the ghost of the queen's father, and he was tormenting her from beyond the grave. She had no one to defend her from him. He was slowly turning the poor woman mad.

"If I could reach through this mirror and kill you myself, I would! You're ugly and vile and your heart is black as night. You repulse me." The queen cried even harder as the man in the mirror continued. "Your daughter, Snow White, is the fairest in the land. I could never love you or find you beautiful while she lives." The queen looked up at her father through swollen, tear-filled eyes. Maleficent thought the queen must be bewitched or under his spell, because she couldn't fathom any other reason the queen would want the horrible man's approval, or want that creature to love her and find her beautiful. It made Maleficent ill.

"Will you love me if I kill Snow White?" the queen asked, an evil smile on her lips.

"Yes, my daughter. That would please me. That would make me love you more."

Maleficent had heard enough. Snow White had been right to be afraid. Something had to be done. Maleficent opened the door, startling the wicked queen, who turned around, ready for a fight. Maleficent raised her hand, using her magic to send the queen flying into the far wall of her chambers. An invisible force left the queen unable to move or speak. The wicked queen was trying to scream, but no sound came from her lips.

"You are a monster for treating your daughter so cruelly!" The evil queen was shocked to see that Maleficent wasn't speaking to her but to her father's reflection in the mirror.

"I condemn you to Hades, where vile and wicked things belong! I banish you from this mirror and from this house, never to revisit it again!" Maleficent cried.

The mirror shattered with an explosive crash that reverberated through the entire castle. She heard Snow White's scream from the courtyard. The young princess ran into the castle and up to her mother's rooms, where she found the queen crying in a heap in Maleficent's arms.

Before Maleficent could tell Snow White that

she and her mother were safe, everything around her melted away. It was the strangest sensation, seeing the queen's castle slowly disappear and the courtyard in the Fairylands appear. The courtyard was cluttered with the eager faces of fairies waiting for the students to come out of exams. Maleficent desperately wanted to stay with the queen and her daughter. She wanted to be sure they would be okay. She wanted to comfort Snow White, to make sure the queen would recover. Surely this wasn't what it was going to be like if she became a wish-granting fairy? She hoped she would have more time with her charges.

Maleficent blinked a few times, adjusting to her new surroundings. She must have been the first to finish the exam, because she didn't see any of the other students. She stood there, trying not to fidget. She was unsure what to do next until Nanny ran up to give her a big hug. "You did beautifully, my darling! Just brilliantly. I am so proud of you."

The Fairy Godmother cleared her throat. "Let's save the comments until everyone has finished.

No sense in getting her hopes up unnecessarily."

Nanny flashed her sister a dirty look. "What do you mean? She did really well."

The Fairy Godmother shook her head. "Of course you would think so, but I think she should have done things differently."

"What should I have done differently? I saved the queen," Maleficent said. But the Fairy Godmother didn't answer her.

Just then, the Blue Fairy appeared next to Maleficent. "How did you do?" Maleficent asked. The Blue Fairy looked concerned she hadn't done well, but Maleficent had a feeling that she had performed the exam beautifully. Soon all the fairies except Flora, Fauna, and Merryweather had appeared. The Fairy Godmother refused to give anyone her results until they returned.

"I wonder if they're okay. Should someone go check on them?" Maleficent asked.

"You would like that, wouldn't you? To have them disqualified?" the Fairy Godmother snapped.

Maleficent was shocked. It was true she didn't

like the three fairies, but she wouldn't want to see them unfairly disqualified. "What do you mean?"

Nanny put her arm around Maleficent's shoulders. "If an instructor has to go into the story, then the fairy is disqualified."

"Can another student go in to help? What if they're in trouble?" Maleficent insisted.

The Fairy Godmother looked at her suspiciously but seemed to be considering the possibility when the three fairies finally appeared.

"Oh, my goodness! Finally! It was so dreadful. I can't believe we made it out alive!" Merryweather said dramatically. Fauna and Flora looked as if they were stricken by some sort of ailment. Maleficent wondered what they had faced in their scenario.

"Are you okay?" she asked them, but the fairies didn't thank her for her concern.

"It's your fault! You attacked us!" Merryweather snapped.

Maleficent was shocked. "I don't understand. What are you talking about?"

"You know exactly what we're talking about, Maleficent!" Merryweather shouted.

"You tried to sabotage us, Maleficent!" Flora screamed.

"I did not!" Maleficent looked at Nanny, confused. "I swear I have no idea what she's talking about!"

Merryweather pointed her finger accusingly at Maleficent. "You know what you did! You attacked us, trying to protect your evil birds!"

Nanny had never seen exams devolve into such chaos, but she did know her daughter had nothing to do with it. "The Fairy Godmother and I will look at your story, and we will figure out what happened," Nanny said.

"I don't think the One of Legends should be able to help decide, even if she is the headmistress!" Merryweather insisted. "She is Maleficent's adoptive mother. She can't be objective!"

Nanny looked at Merryweather, wondering where they had gone wrong with that one. How had she let those three fairies become so petty? Had she spent so much time trying to lift up Maleficent that she had neglected those three, leaving them to her sister? She suddenly felt responsible for those fairies and wondered why she hadn't taken the time to guide them and set them on the path of goodness that she had thought was their fate. She searched within herself and through time to see how the three would end up. In spite of their pettiness, she saw goodness, kindness, and pure hearts. There would be squabbling, and perhaps a bit of bullying on Merryweather's part, but she saw her pushing the other two because they needed guidance. She saw there was a child they would care for deeply, a child who would need their protection. She sighed with relief, knowing she hadn't failed them entirely. However, that didn't change who they were today—three petty girls hurling insults at her and her daughter.

"Girls, please! I won't be deciding who passes or fails. But I imagine you'd be very pleased if I did. I see an important task for you in the future, a task you will not be able to accomplish without wish-granting status," Nanny said.

The three fairies looked at each other in disbelief.

"And I promise we will look into this matter of Maleficent attacking you," Nanny finished.

The Fairy Godmother cleared her throat. She didn't like her sister taking things over, so she took the matter in hand herself. "I suggest everyone go back home and have some tea. We will interview the charges and decide who will be granted status. We will make the announcement later today. I know you are all eager for the results. We promise to make our decision as soon as we can."

Maleficent looked at her mother with worried eyes, her skin turning a pale shade of purple. "My darling, don't fret. Go home. The odd sisters are there waiting for you," Nanny told her.

Maleficent kissed her mother on the cheek and did as she was asked. She followed all the other students filing out of the courtyard to go home and wait for the exam results.

The Fairy Godmother quickly got to business. With her wand, she conjured up a little round table with a dark pink tablecloth that matched the cherry blossoms behind them. She also conjured two white chairs with pink cushions to match. "Sit, Sister. Sit!" And with another wave of her wand, a teapot, teacups with saucers, and little plates, all a pale shade of pink, edged in glistening silver, appeared on the table. "Have some tea, Sister, before it gets cold. Oh! And I almost forgot!" With another wave of her wand, little white cakes decorated with pink roses settled on the plates. "There! Now we're ready." Nanny laughed to herself, but she let her sister talk. "We'll discuss each student in order of completion of the exam. Does that sound fair?"

Nanny nodded, letting her sister speak first. "I'm sure you'll agree that Maleficent did deplorably. She failed to realize her charge was actually Princess Snow White, not the wicked queen."

Nanny scoffed. "So what do you suppose Maleficent should have done? Let the queen languish in torment and try to kill her own daughter?

There was no fairy, no good sorceress to help Snow White. There was no other part for Maleficent to play in this scenario than to destroy the man in the mirror! She saved the queen *and* the princess! You can't deny it!"

The Fairy Godmother was shaking her head furiously the entire time her sister was speaking. Nanny felt anger growing inside her. "You know as well as I that the three fairies chosen should be Maleficent, the Blue Fairy, and your favorites, Flora, Fauna, and Merryweather. Do we really need to sit here and debate this all day?"

Just then, the odd sisters flew into the courtyard, screaming at the top of their lungs like wild harpies. Ruby was holding the hand of a small blond girl. The tiny girl seemed to be made of all things silver and gold, shining like a star. She was crying so hard she was shaking. "Where are those little beasts? Where is Merryweather, where are her friends?" Ruby shrieked.

Maleficent ran into the courtyard just behind them. "Where are my birds? Where is my crow tree?"

The little blond girl continued to sob.

"Maleficent! You're frightening this young girl. Stop this screaming at once!" scolded the Fairy Godmother.

Lucinda glared at her. "It was your fairies who made our Circe cry! Not Maleficent! Merryweather attacked her!"

Nanny rushed over to Circe and the odd sisters. "Circe, what happened? Merryweather attacked you?"

"All three of them attacked me, but I think it was my fault," she sobbed.

"What happened?" Nanny asked in her gentlest voice, hoping to calm not only Circe but also the odd sisters and Maleficent, who were equally outraged.

"When the three fairies appeared on their path, I saw into their hearts. I saw they had a terrible secret. They had taken Maleficent's raven, Diablo, and hidden him away so she would worry and fret over him. They wanted Maleficent to be distracted at her exam today. I didn't think it was fair, so I took the form of Maleficent to see if they would help me find her raven. But no matter how much I begged them for help, they refused to even look at me." Circe was crying so hard now she couldn't keep telling the story.

"How did Merryweather know Maleficent was taking the exam today?" asked Nanny, giving her sister an angry look. "Did you tell them?"

The Fairy Godmother couldn't bring herself to meet her sister's gaze. "I might have said something to Merryweather after the argument you and I had in your kitchen." Nanny was incensed, but the Fairy Godmother kept talking. "But I didn't have anything to do with *this*!"

"Stop your insipid squabbling and let our sister finish her story!" screeched Martha.

"Tell them what happened next, dear," Ruby said encouragingly, holding Circe's hand in hers.

"I . . . I . . . decided to appear further along the path. I was in the middle of a beautiful forest, standing beneath the largest of the trees there. I was still disguised as Maleficent, weeping because I couldn't find Diablo and Opal. The fairies didn't realize that

I wasn't the real Maleficent. They started screaming at me, accusing me of trying to ruin their exam. They hurled silver sparks at me, which made the crow tree catch on fire." Circe sobbed even more. "I didn't know! I didn't know the birds were in the tree. I didn't know the fairies had hidden them there from Maleficent. I thought it was all make-pretend!"

"And where are Maleficent's birds now?" Nanny asked, her heart full of fear.

Circe collapsed in a heap of tears. "I'm so sorry! I didn't mean to put Maleficent's pets in danger! I didn't realize the fairies would try to hurt us!"

The odd sisters took their little sister in their arms and held her tightly as she cried. "It's not your fault, my dear! You didn't know. Maleficent won't blame you. It's not your fault. It's not your fault!"

"Where are Maleficent's birds?" Nanny asked again, frantically searching everyone's faces for answers they didn't have. "Maleficent, where are your birds?"

Maleficent was crying. "I don't know. My crow tree isn't in our yard."

Nanny was trying to stay calm. "Circe, darling, are you sure it was the real Opal and Diablo with you in the scene?"

Circe nodded. "I am!"

Nanny waved her hand, summoning Merry-weather, Fauna, and Flora. The fairies were surprised to find themselves standing in front of a legion of angry witches. "Where are Diablo and Opal? Where are Maleficent's birds?" Nanny asked sternly.

The three fairies looked frightened and began speaking all at once. "We didn't mean for them to be harmed, I swear! We didn't realize that our charge would turn herself into Maleficent and threaten us! We thought she was Maleficent! We thought she was angry because we had stolen her precious birds!"

Maleficent stopped crying, her face turning a startling shade of green. She just stared at the fairies. She was deathly quiet and seething with anger. The fairies almost wished she would scream at them. Her silence was unsettling.

"Maleficent, I'm sorry! We would never hurt your birds on purpose," Flora whimpered.

Maleficent quietly stretched out her arms, the sleeves of her robes resembling a raven's wings. *"Where are my birds?"*

The three fairies gasped with fright. "We don't know! We promise! We swear!"

Maleficent's face became stone cold and her yellow eyes blazed. *"Lies!* Where are my birds? Tell me *now!"*

"No! Not until you stand down and renounce your right to wish granting!" Merryweather shouted. "We can't have you sullying the good name of the fairies in this land by spreading your filth to the many kingdoms!"

"That's enough!" Nanny yelled. "Tell us where you have put Maleficent's birds or I will punish you myself!"

"You will not touch them, Sister!" the Fairy Godmother said, stepping in front of the three fairies. "When will you give up this wretched girl? When will you see that Maleficent will bring you nothing but pain and misery? You saw it the night you brought her home, when you looked through her time in this world. You saw it through to the end, but still you insisted on taking her in. You cared for her and defended her even though she doesn't deserve it!"

"What is she talking about?" Maleficent's anger was turning into heartbreak.

"Nothing, my dear, nothing," Nanny said.

Maleficent began crying again. "What is she talking about? What did you see? Am I evil? Is that why I was abandoned?"

"Yes! You were created in *evil*, and you will do *evil* to the end of your days. You will destroy *everything* you have ever loved!" yelled the Fairy Godmother.

"No, Maleficent, don't listen to her. It's not true!" Nanny insisted.

Maleficent's fingertips started to tingle. The terrible feeling quickly spread to the rest of her body, turning into a burning sensation that came from within. She remembered feeling that way when she was younger, before she had learned to teleport to her tree house, before she had learned how to control her anger. But this time—this time it felt different. This time *she* was different.

"Maleficent, *no!*" Nanny screamed.

Everything in Maleficent's world went black as she became unbearably hot. It felt as if the raging heat burning uncontrollably inside her would consume her. But just when she was sure the heat would make her burst, she felt herself expanding, becoming larger and more imposing, as if her body was making room for her anger. The heat that had been growing within her was creating space for the pain, the heartache, and the betrayal she felt at hearing that Nanny had seen she would become evil. How could she have lied to her all that time? How could she have kept that from her? This awful thing inside her now raged like a beast. It was like a hungry serpent eating away at her insides, devouring her. She screamed in pain, her cries mingling with her mother's screams until she could no longer tell the difference between the two. She couldn't bear it. It was the most terrible thing she'd ever experienced. She lost all sense of herself as a blinding green fire exploded from within her, destroying everything in her path.

And all she could think was they had all been right.

She *was* evil.

CHAPTER XXIII

'NANNY'S REGRET

The room was eerily quiet. There were tears in everyone's eyes except Maleficent's. After a moment, she broke the silence. "But you didn't die. None of you did. I thought I had killed my mother and everyone I had ever known. I didn't find out until later that you had survived."

"If it hadn't been for the odd sisters' spiriting us away, we *would* have died," Nanny said softly.

"I suppose they knew what happened was a possibility. I suppose you all did. Everything the odd sisters said the night before my birthday about the stars not aligning made sense after that. I fulfilled my destiny that day."

"Yes, we knew it was possible *something* disastrous might happen. . . ."

"Did you know I would turn into a dragon and destroy the Fairylands? Is that what you and your sister saw when you found me in that tree?"

"No! I never saw that, I swear! I knew you were capable of great evil, but I had faith you would take another path. I always saw the good within you, Maleficent," Nanny insisted.

Maleficent turned her steely gaze to Circe. "You've been awfully quiet, listening from your sisters' enchanted mirror, Circe. Have you nothing to say?"

Circe hesitated before replying. "I was a child, Maleficent. I don't even recall visiting the Fairylands. I don't remember meeting you, the three good fairies, or the Fairy Godmother. I'm sorry for whatever part I might have played in what happened, I really am, but it sounds as if I was trying to defend you."

Maleficent contemplated Circe's words. "You truly don't remember?"

Circe shook her head. "I don't."

Maleficent smirked. "Then it would seem you're almost the same girl you were then. *Almost*, but not quite."

Circe didn't understand the Dark Fairy's meaning, but she decided not to press it. All of this seemed so unreal. Circe had heard many tales of the villainous Maleficent. It was strange to hear the story of her as a hopeful girl—to hear tales of her own sisters as they lay helpless in the solarium. And her sisters were now too close to the Dark Fairy for Circe's liking. She suddenly felt foolish for leaving the castle while so many she loved were at risk. Her head was spinning. Circe felt as if she were trapped in a nightmare, a mixed-up fairy tale, and she couldn't tell how it would end.

"What happened to Diablo and your crows? Were they hurt?" Tulip asked, drawing Maleficent's attention away from Circe.

Maleficent shook her head. "No, they are all still with me to this day."

"But what happened to them? How did they find you?" Circe asked.

"Luckily, they weren't hurt by my destruction of the Fairylands. They were trapped in the alternate reality created for the fairy exams. I thought you would know this, Circe. You must have been with your sisters when they found my birds. Your sisters were the ones who moved everyone in the Fairylands to the alternate reality when they realized I was transforming. They knew they would be safe there."

"I told you, I have no memory of what happened, Maleficent," Circe insisted. "In fact, I have no memories of my childhood whatsoever. My sisters would never talk to me about that time."

Maleficent regarded her like a cat eyeing a mouse. "Is that so?"

Maleficent lifted her gaze to Nanny, who was holding the mirror. Nanny studied her daughter. She could no longer detect any love in Maleficent's heart. It was as if a part of Maleficent was missing. The part Nanny had loved so much was somehow gone, ripped from Maleficent's being. And Nanny couldn't bring herself to ask her how she lost it.

"Why did you let me believe I had killed you?"

Maleficent asked, pulling Nanny from her thoughts. Her yellow eyes were blazing, and her skin had turned a light shade of green.

"I didn't know that was what you thought!" Nanny said.

"Why didn't you at least try to find me? I was your daughter! And you didn't even try to find out if I was living or dead."

"I did! I searched everywhere for you. I could not find you, I swear! I thought you had died, consumed by the flames. It took me and my sister an age to restore the Fairylands. You destroyed everything, Maleficent—and almost everyone. It took all my power and strength to bring life back into that place. It wasn't until the odd sisters told me they had found you alive, years later, that I learned you still lived."

"You're a powerful witch. Had you wanted to find me, you would have! How could you not feel me in the world? Even in my dragon form!" Maleficent spat.

"You stayed a dragon? For how long, Maleficent?"

"For years," Maleficent croaked.

She said nothing more, but Nanny finally understood. She hadn't been able find Maleficent because she had remained a dragon. She hadn't felt her moving in the world because Maleficent hadn't been herself. "I'm so sorry you were by yourself all those years, Maleficent."

"I had my birds." Maleficent's words were like a knife in Nanny's heart. The thought of her little fairy alone for so many years shattered her.

Maleficent waved her hand. "It's no matter. I'm content with my life, with my power and what I've achieved. I am the mistress of all evil, as prophesied by you and your sister!"

Nanny was hurt. "I never saw that for you!"

"*Lies!* You knew from the moment you saw me I was evil. You gave me everything I needed to become who I am!"

"Don't you see it was my sister who caused this? Listening to you just now, I could tell it was her words. She brought about this prophecy!"

"Yes, blame everything on your sister, as always,"

Maleficent sneered. "You never take responsibility for your own actions. And I suppose you will say it was she who decided to have Merryweather and her friends care for Aurora and who decided the child's fate?"

"What should it matter to you who cared for Aurora?" Circe asked, feeling protective of Nanny.

Maleficent's expression turned as hard as stone. "Your sisters didn't warn you, did they? Well, let me make it plain for you, and never make me repeat it again. Never question me about the child. Ever! There was a time when I loved your sisters well, but that love will not protect you!"

In that moment Circe realized the magnitude of Maleficent's rage. She meant what she said; her words were like a spell woven in pure hatred. Her anger was a bubbling inferno inside her, just waiting to come out.

But Nanny saw something else at the mention of Aurora; another emotion had surfaced and overwhelmed her anger: concern. It was like a shining star in the darkness. Nanny could see that this one star had guided Maleficent over the years, even as she had become more corrupt and stopped being the person Nanny remembered. That one aspect had prevailed: her obsession with the child and her relentless need to keep her asleep.

This time it was Circe who interrupted Nanny's thoughts. "I'm sorry, Maleficent, but if I'm not mistaken, you need my help. Mine and Nanny's, correct? Might I suggest you stop threatening me, and then maybe we can make some progress?"

Maleficent flashed her yellow eyes at Circe, mildly impressed that the pretty little witch didn't seem to be intimidated by her. "You've been raised well, Circe. You are a very powerful witch, though you have much compassion in your heart. That may eventually be your downfall. But I'm happy to see you have your wits about you, unlike your deranged mothers."

"You mean my sisters," Circe said, correcting her.

"No, I mean your mothers," Maleficent smirked.

"You lie just to hurt her, Maleficent!" Nanny

said, raising her voice with Maleficent for the first time since she had arrived.

Maleficent drew back. "I may be the mistress of all evil, but I do not lie. *You* are the queen of lies, queen of secrets, queen of betrayal, not I!" Maleficent's voice reverberated through the castle like a malevolent storm.

"What is she talking about?" Circe asked Nanny. But Nanny didn't know. Clearly the odd sisters had secrets they'd shared only with Maleficent.

"You can find the spell in your sisters' books for yourself. It's all right there. How they did it. How they created you," Maleficent said. "You may be the only thing in this world left of them now that they are trapped within the realm of dreams."

"I don't believe they are my mothers. I don't!" Circe cried.

Maleficent laughed. "You know I'm telling the truth! Read the books sitting before you. Everything is there. Learn your mothers' secrets now that their books are open to you. I gave them the spells that protected their secrets from you all this time. But they no longer inhabit this world. Those spells are broken! Why do you think you have always had greater power than them? Why do you think they have always deferred to you, their *little sister*? *You* are *them!* But go! Go look for yourself. When you find the book that tells you their secrets and mine, secrets we have been hiding, you bring those secrets back here. Bring them to me and to the One of Legends, and then you will know what I say is true. Only then will you want to help me!"

Circe's reflection in the mirror looked at Nanny, wondering what she should do.

"Go, my dear. Do as she says!" Nanny said. "See for yourself and bring the book back to the castle."

Nanny looked at Tulip and Popinjay. "My sweet dears, I have not forgotten you. Tulip, can you and Popinjay please go attend to that matter we discussed earlier?"

"Yes, of course, Nanny," Tulip said. She had almost forgotten that they were expecting the Fairy Godmother and the three good fairies.

"Directing everyone like a maestro as usual, I see," Maleficent snapped.

"Stop this, Maleficent," Nanny cried. "Have you not heard anything I've said to you? I loved you! I loved you more than anyone I have ever known. I loved you as my own child. I still do. Please stop this condemnation!"

Tulip and Popinjay felt like they were eavesdropping on a personal conversation. They crept out of the room as quietly as they could without disrupting mother and daughter, because that was what Nanny and Maleficent were. Mother and daughter.

Or at least they had been at one time.

CHAPTER XXIV

POPINJAY'S
WILD RIDE

Tulip closed the door softly behind them as they slipped into the corridor. Hudson was standing nearby, as usual, waiting to assist Nanny or Tulip.

"Hudson, please go downstairs and rest," Tulip said. "There is no need for you to stand here. If Nanny needs you, she will ring. You have been on your feet for days. You're going to make yourself ill. Please, do as I say, and take care."

Hudson put on a brave face, but he was relieved by the permission to take his repose. "If there is nothing else I can do for you, Princess, then I think I will go do just that."

"Thank you, Hudson," Tulip replied. "When you get downstairs, please tell Violet tea is expected in the garden for five. I will be entertaining guests from the Fairylands."

"Yes, Princess," Hudson replied, and he set off into the great bowels of the castle, where the servants lived and worked. It occurred to Tulip that every castle was like a great ship, and this one had Hudson at the helm. She hoped everyone in every house throughout the many lands had a Hudson to take charge during harrowing times.

"Will you be okay, Tulip?" Popinjay had his hand on Tulip's arm and was smiling at her. He was feeling proud that she loved him.

"I will be fine, my love. I promise we can handle this." She looked at Popinjay for a long moment, taking in his beautiful gray eyes, and sighed. "You know I love you, Popinjay," she said, and Popinjay blushed. Tulip wished their courtship hadn't been born in this wild maelstrom, but there was nothing to be done about it. She was just happy that

Popinjay seemed more than willing to take this wild ride with her, without complaint and without fretting over her. She was happy to have him by her side, and Popinjay seemed happy to be there.

CHAPTER XXV

THE ODD SISTERS' SECRET

Circe's mind was reeling after hearing Maleficent's story and what the Dark Fairy had said about her sisters really being her mothers. *How is that possible?* She needed to get fresh air—to get out of her sisters' house. She needed time to think and to breathe.

Circe stepped outside and saw a woman headed in her direction. She wore a lightweight black taffeta dress, which moved delicately with the woman's small gestures. The dress was bejeweled with ruby-red apples and featured an embroidered tree accented with fine golden-threaded little birds. "Queen Snow White?" Circe cried. She had nearly forgotten that the queen was on her way.

"Hello! Yes," the woman called out. She made her way to Circe with a broad smile on her face.

"Hello, Your Majesty!" Circe said. "I was so happy when you wrote to say you would come. I wasn't sure if you would."

Snow White smiled at Circe. "Please, call me Snow. Of course I wanted to come. I wanted to bring you the book right away." Snow smiled, and the lines around her eyes deepened, making her even more beautiful to Circe. "I could tell from your kind letter you're very different from your sisters."

Snow White stopped walking and looked at Circe with a puzzled expression on her face. She was trying to connect Circe to the odd sisters from her childhood memories. Snow couldn't imagine this woman being related to those horrible women. Then, suddenly, something fell into place for Snow. "Wait, Circe. You're the enchantress who cursed the Beast Prince?"

"Yes, I am." Circe cast down her eyes in shame. She hated to be making that impression on her new-found cousin.

"Well, aren't you brilliant? I think I've already decided I like you very much, Circe," Snow said as she looped her arm through Circe's. "From what I understand, he was a beastly person and deserved every bit of that curse!"

The ladies laughed and Circe felt more at ease in the company of her cousin. "Please come inside. I will make you a cup of tea," she said.

"Since you're familiar with the Beast Prince's story," Circe said, "this is where Ursula found Princess Tulip, right there beneath the surface of the water, after Tulip jumped from these cliffs. It hurts my heart to think Tulip was so heartbroken over that wretched man. But the entire experience really did help her become the amazing young woman she is now, so I shouldn't lament the path that brought her here."

As Snow listened, her large dark eyes seemed to sparkle with some thought she wasn't sharing. It occurred to Circe that Snow White was a quiet woman. She knew she already loved Snow White, even though she had met her only a few moments before. There was an undeniable kindness within her that endeared her to Circe.

"You don't talk very much, do you, Snow?"

Snow shook her head. "I suppose not. I talk with my mother, my daughters, and with my husband, the king, of course. They are my best friends."

Circe could hear what Snow White wasn't saying. *My mother is protective. She doesn't like me traveling to other kingdoms. She doesn't like me to keep company with people she doesn't know or trust.* "Well, I assure you, Snow, you are safe with me. You can trust me."

Snow smiled at Circe. "I believe I can."

The ladies smiled at each other, feeling lucky to be in each other's company. And because she felt comfortable with Snow, Circe shared Maleficent's news with her.

"So . . ." Snow began, giving Circe a concerned look. "Do you think Maleficent was telling the truth about your sisters? You seem unsure."

Circe paused at the foot of the little stairway

that led to the front door of the odd sisters' house. She thought about the question. "I don't know," she replied finally, taking a small pouch from her pocket.

Circe sprinkled a brilliant sapphire-colored powder out of the pouch into Snow's hand. It sparkled in the sunlight, as though it were made of real sapphires. "Now blow, in that direction," Circe said, pointing.

Snow did as Circe instructed. Suddenly, a house appeared before her eyes. She felt foolish for gasping, but she couldn't help it. The spell had astounded her.

Snow marveled at the odd sisters' house. She had never seen one quite like it before. She had never thought much about where the odd sisters lived. She'd always thought they just popped out of a deep black vortex when they decided it was time to torment their victims, and then disappeared back into the void in a puff of smoke when they were done. That is, until they were ready for more skullduggery with another victim. But their house really was charming. The roof even resembled a witch's cap.

When she walked through the door into a bright, airy kitchen that featured a large round window, she couldn't help noticing the apple tree right outside. "Is that . . ."

Circe pursed her lips, feeling foolish for not obscuring the tree. "I'm afraid so. My sisters have artifacts from all their, um . . . adventures."

Snow frowned. "I'd hardly call tormenting my family an adventure." But Snow understood it was likely a word Circe used as a form of denial. Snow had often employed similar terms herself when referring to her mother as different women, even though the woman she loved and knew now was the same one who had tried to kill her, no matter how much she tried to separate them in her mind.

Hearing Snow's thoughts, Circe sighed. "Exactly. I'm so happy we understand each other. Probably even more than we could possibly know now. I have a feeling we are going to be great friends. I already love you very much."

Snow White smiled. "I feel the same way. After everything you've told me, I feel as though I already know you quite well. And you've shared so much with me, everything you've been through these past few days . . . I feel as if I've experienced it with you. It's so strange being here—being in your sisters' house. I spent so many years wondering who your sisters really were. Wondering what made them the way they are and why they hounded me as a child. They still haunt me in my dreams."

Circe looked concerned. "Do they? I'm so sorry. If they are sending you bad dreams, I will see what I can do to put a stop to it."

Now Circe had another reason to be upset with her sisters. After all those years, they were still tormenting Snow White. It made her angrier than she wanted to admit. "Come, sit down and make yourself comfortable. I will make you some tea," Circe said. She could tell Snow didn't quite understand why she was there.

It had suddenly occurred to Snow that she could

214

have just sent the book. Why had she come? Was it presumptuous of her to intrude like this with Circe going through so much?

Circe smiled at her cousin. "I did send you the spell so you could come, Snow. You're most welcome here."

Snow handed Circe the book of fairy tales she had brought with her. "Here, take this. And let me make the tea. I can't stand not feeling useful. Since I don't know my way around spell books, you should probably leave the more mundane tasks, like making tea and preparing meals, to me."

Circe thought Snow White was probably the sweetest lady she had ever met. She had almost forgotten Snow was a queen. "You probably have people who do these things for you."

Snow laughed harder than she had in a while. "I used to handle cooking and cleaning for seven dwarfs. I can handle making us a pot of tea. I know you're eager to look through your sisters' spell books and the book of fairy tales. And I know you can't possibly be comfortable leaving Nanny alone with Maleficent for too long, even if it's what she wants. So you'd better get to work."

Circe smiled at Snow's thoughtfulness. Circe didn't doubt Nanny's ability to protect herself, but she knew Nanny's heart. She couldn't imagine Nanny hurting Maleficent, even in self-defense. Setting Snow's fairy tale book to the side, she opened one of her sisters' spell books.

As Snow looked through the odd sisters' kitchen cabinet for teacups, she came across a beautiful deep blue one edged in metallic gold. Something about it reminded her of her childhood. She was almost certain that her mother had had teacups just like it. Snow almost mentioned something to Circe, but she didn't want to bother her while she was searching.

"Oh, gods! I think they really are my mothers!" Circe cried. She was becoming frantic. Something within filled her with dread, causing Circe's heart to pound so fast she thought she might faint.

"Circe, are you okay? What is it? Did you find something?" Snow asked, concerned.

"No, I'm sorry I'm such a mess. I'm worried Maleficent is telling the truth, and it's giving me anxiety," Circe admitted.

"Is there anything I can do for you? Do you need some water?" Snow's sweet voice rang out like a little bell.

Circe looked at her cousin. "I'm just so overwhelmed, Snow. I honestly don't know where to begin looking in all these books. My head is spinning."

Snow joined Circe on the floor. She placed her small hand on her cousin's shoulder. "You're in shock, Circe. Take a moment to breathe. Why don't you start by looking for journals dated before you were born? You said Maleficent mentioned something about your sisters also keeping a secret of hers. Maybe you should look for journals that concern her."

Circe was thankful for the suggestions. "And you wondered why you came here. Thank you."

Snow smiled and brought Circe her tea.

"What's on your mind, Snow?" Circe asked.

Snow laughed. "Can't you tell?"

Circe shook her head. "Not always. Not if I'm not listening. I do get the sense you wanted to ask me something. Something you think might upset me."

"I'm wondering if you're going to wake up your sisters."

"I . . . well . . . of course I am," Circe said. But she herself was starting to wonder if that was really a good idea.

"You don't seem sure."

Circe wondered if Snow was reading *her* thoughts. "Are my expressions that easy to read?"

Snow put back the deep blue and shining gold teacup, deciding she didn't fancy being reminded of her childhood. Instead, she chose two cups that were black and edged in silver. "Well, if I were you, I would be feeling the same way. I'd be conflicted. Part of me would want my family back, but the other would wonder if it was responsible to unleash them on the many kingdoms."

Circe knew what she was saying was true. "And

of course, if Maleficent is telling the truth, and I have a feeling she is, I will want answers. Answers only my mothers will have."

"And you will want those answers from them directly? You don't think you will find all the answers you need in these books?" Snow brought Circe her cup of tea as Circe started a fire in the fireplace with a wave of her hand.

"I'm not sure," Circe replied. "But there's only one way to find out."

✤ ✤ ✤ ✤

As Circe searched through her sisters' books, Snow sat in one of the love seats, sipping her tea and letting her thoughts wander. Strangely, she felt a sense of relief to be away from her mother. She was happy to be in this house with her new friend and happy to be on her own for the first time in her life. Ever since she was very small, Snow had been in the company of someone she had to take care of: her father after her mother had died, and her stepmother after her father had died. It had continued with the dwarfs when she was hiding from her mother, and of course her own children had depended upon her when they were growing up, but that had been Snow's greatest pleasure and not a burden. And now that her children were grown, it was her mother who always seemed to need constant assurance of Snow's love. It was true her mother protected her, sheltered her, and enchanted the lands around her so that she would always be happy. But Snow realized now, after some time away from her, that she was really the one taking care of her mother. She was always comforting her, making her feel better. Always making the old queen feel less guilty for the things she'd done to her when she was younger. It was exhausting.

Circe could hear the thoughts running through Snow's mind, and she could relate. She imagined the scene that would likely transpire if she was able to wake her sisters. All the guilt and anguish for her part in how they ended up in the land of dreams would rain upon her head. Circe sometimes forgot how angry she could be with her sisters because of the horrible things they'd done. Sometimes she forgot that her anger with them was justified.

She didn't share her thoughts with Snow, because she felt they already understood each other. She wondered if that would all be ruined once her sisters woke up. Her sisters had no love for Snow White, though Circe didn't understand why. Often her sisters' hatred was arbitrary, and surely that was the case with Snow White. She had been just a child when they knew her. *Perhaps I will find answers in these journals. Maybe after all these years, I will finally get to know my sisters and learn who they really are.*

She had been looking through the spell books for a long while when something finally caught her eye. Circe went ghastly pale. All the color ran from her face and she looked like she might faint. "Oh, Snow! I think I found it! I think I found what Maleficent was talking about. It's a spell!"

"What is it?" Snow ran to Circe. "Are you okay? Come sit down over here. I will get you some more water. You look dreadful."

Circe was in shock. "I understand now. It all makes sense. Everything. Every foul deed. My sisters' mania. My powers. Everything."

"What does it say?" Snow's eyes were wide. She was frightened for Circe. Before Circe could answer, they were interrupted by a terrible rumbling.

Snow rushed to the window and saw that the house was lifting off the cliff, rising through the clouds into the heavens. "Circe! What's happening? Are you doing this?"

Circe looked just as terrified as Snow was. "No, I don't know why the house is traveling! Snow, sit down. I'm sure we'll be safe, but please sit down, just in case."

Circe went to the large round window in the kitchen to get a better view of where they were headed. Although she had experienced it more times than she could correctly recall, her sisters had always directed the house. She had no idea why it was moving on its own.

Snow clenched the arms of her chair tightly.

Circe sat back down beside Snow. "We'll be fine, sweetheart. I promise. This is the way my sisters and I have always traveled. The house is meant to move from one place to another like this. I just don't understand why it's happening now and on its own."

"But where are we going, Circe?" Snow asked.

"I don't know, my dear. I guess we'll find out when we get there."

CHAPTER XXVI

MOTHERS AND DAUGHTERS

Nanny had never imagined sitting with Maleficent like this again, just talking.

"I wish I knew what you were thinking. I always did," Maleficent said.

"You seem much changed to me, Maleficent," Nanny replied. "There are so many things I want to know, so many things I want to say to you, but there isn't much time."

"What could you possibly say to me now that would make a difference?" Maleficent snapped.

Nanny paused for a moment. "I could tell you that I understand."

Maleficent stood, her rage burning within her.

"There is no way you could possibly understand! Do you know how I spent those years after I destroyed the Fairylands? After I was finally myself again and no longer in my dragon form?" Maleficent asked.

Nanny shook her head.

"I was alone, tortured by the thought that I had killed you!" Maleficent's rage knocked Nanny back like a blow to her chest. It felt hot and vile. Nanny was worried that Maleficent was about to lose control. It must have shown on Nanny's face, because Maleficent cackled manically. "Oh, don't worry; I won't burn down your precious Tulip's castle. I can control my powers now. Nothing will burn. Not unless I want it to."

Nanny didn't find that knowledge reassuring. "Maleficent, listen to me, I couldn't find you, I swear. I searched everywhere. I used every kind of magic I could to seek you out. I mourned you sincerely, because I thought you had died when you destroyed the Fairylands. I thought your rage had consumed you. You have no idea how much I suffered over the loss of you."

Maleficent shook her head violently. "But when you learned she was alive, you didn't come to her. Your daughter! The odd sisters told you they'd found her, and you didn't come! You didn't come for her! You left her alone in that ruined castle."

"You mean I left *you* alone in that castle. I didn't come to *you*."

"That girl, your daughter, she doesn't exist! She's dead because you abandoned her!"

"I was afraid," Nanny admitted. "It wasn't until the odd sisters came to me for help with the little princess that I knew what you had been going through. But then I had Aurora to consider. She was small and defenseless, like you had once been. She needed a home. And she needed someone to care for her and love her."

"So you put her in the hands of the three good fairies? You gave my daughter to them! How could you?"

Nanny was shocked. "Your daughter? How is that possible? Is that true?"

"Don't pretend like you didn't know! Of course

you knew! You know everything. Tell me you didn't guess. Tell me you didn't know in the back of your mind that she was mine. Be honest with me and with yourself for once!" Maleficent bellowed. "You gave her to them. To *them*! Those foul fairies! Those horrible creatures who loathe me! You gave my daughter to *them*!"

Nanny felt terrible. She'd failed Maleficent more than she had known. Nanny realized that Maleficent could never forgive her, no matter how much she pleaded with her. "I didn't have a choice! I saw it the day of the exams. I saw that the good fairies would take care of a little girl whom they would grow to love very much. She was their charge, Maleficent. It was ordained. I can't control the order of succession. I can't change what is written in the book of fairies. You know this! You know it better than any fairy!"

"Why couldn't you have given her to the Blue Fairy? To anyone other than *them*?"

"You know the Blue Fairy has her own charge— the little boy. Flora, Fauna, and Merryweather were next in line. I'm sorry, Maleficent, but there was no way around it. All abandoned children with destinies of their own are given to a fairy. This is a fairy's primary duty. And besides, if you hadn't cursed her to die, cursed this child you call your own, the good fairies wouldn't have had to stay in her life. Their involvement would have ended the day they gave her to King Stefan and his queen, the day of her christening! You caused the fairies to take her away into the forest and change her name. You did that with your curse. This is not my fault, Maleficent. You have brought this on yourself!"

"You could have taken her case! You could have stepped in!" Maleficent shouted. "You were always Oberon's favorite. No one would have questioned you. You could have done that for me! You could have cared for her yourself! My goodness, in a way, she is your granddaughter."

Nanny was stunned. "What do you mean my granddaughter? Where did you get Aurora? Is she your true daughter? Or did you find her?"

"The odd sisters didn't tell you? You really don't know?" Maleficent's face became very still.

She looked like an animal considering her prey as she tried to decide if Nanny was telling the truth. Nanny couldn't hear Maleficent's thoughts. She had no idea what she was thinking. Her face revealed nothing, no emotion, not even anger.

Maleficent smirked. "I've been practicing keeping my thoughts from you. I see that it's working. For too long, you invaded my mind. For too long, you tried to steer me onto the course you thought I should take. All the while you knew we would end up here. In this place. In this time. As enemies."

"I am not your enemy, Maleficent. You are."

"You dare say that to me? Am I just another vain, power-hungry fool flinging herself into danger? Don't insult me! You have no idea the pain I endured—what I went through."

"Tell me."

Maleficent was taken aback. "What?"

"Tell me what you went through. I want to hear it."

Nanny desperately wanted Maleficent to forgive her, not just for her sake but for Maleficent's.

Oberon was still waiting outside, and she wanted to buy Maleficent more time. To give her a chance to redeem herself. Nanny wanted the tiny star in Maleficent's heart to guide her to redemption. To lead her away from the darkness.

Then maybe, just maybe, Oberon would spare her life.

CHAPTER XXVII

THE DARK FAIRY IN EXILE

"The first memory I have of the place I now call home is sitting on my cold stone throne. I remember shivering in pain, but I felt I deserved it. My only comfort was my ravens and crows. If it weren't for them, I don't know what would have become of me. You have to understand I'm speaking of how I felt then, not how I feel now. I was a different person then. Now everything feels detached.

"Have you ever looked back on events that happened many years ago and felt as if they happened to someone else entirely? That is how I feel now, except the detachment is more profound, because truly I was another person. I have memories of my feelings, of how I felt in the past, but I truly don't think I feel anything now, except rage and the undeniable need to protect my daughter.

"I found my crumbling castle quite by mistake and decided to make it my home. It was inhabited by foul little creatures that feared me. They had seen me in my dragon form and decided I was sent there by their former ruler, Hades, to rule over them in his stead. I found out later my castle was once a great place of power, and the little creatures, who were to become my goons, had been left there, abandoned by Hades when he fled those lands. I never saw the god of the underworld. He didn't visit me, but my birds told me the story relayed to them by the creatures. I spent many years there, alone, suffering over what I had done. I felt I deserved all the pain I was experiencing, and I became very fearful of ever becoming angry again, fearful that I might destroy myself in the process. The pain involved in becoming a dragon is unbearable. I honestly didn't think I would survive it again. It's why I stayed a dragon for so long. I was afraid of the pain involved in transforming back to my true self. And I was afraid of who I would become once I took my true form. Eventually I became lonely and tired of always fighting off some young man who wanted to prove his bravery by killing the great dragon. But it was really the hope of seeing Diablo, Opal, and my birds again that gave me the courage to become myself. I had been without them for so long. My loneliness was palpable. It ate away at me, leaving me with little hope that once I was myself again, they would at last hear my call. But they did. And when I transformed, I found I was very much the same person I was before. I was the fairy you knew and loved, except I was filled with an unspeakable sadness and a tremendous guilt for what I thought I had done to you and to everyone else. As the years passed and my loneliness deepened, I wished you had never found me in that crow tree. I wished I'd never known what it was like to be loved by someone. In those years, my pain and longing for you was so desperate that it rivaled the agony of my dragon transformation. I spent my days practicing magic and reading the books my crows brought to me, spirited away from far-off places. I had my books, my crows, and my ravens. I honestly didn't feel I needed anything else.

"That is, until the odd sisters found me. They had lost their little sister, Circe, and they were deeply saddened. No matter how much I questioned them, they wouldn't say what had happened. They seemed to be consumed with guilt and heartbreak. I imagined they lost her in some manner in which they were at fault. I didn't know the details and I didn't ask. I was just happy they found me. I'd always imagined if they'd somehow survived what had happened in the Fairylands and managed to find me, I would be met with their condemnation and anger, but they came to me with love and concern. They wanted to care for me. They wanted to make me their own and to help me.

"As you know, I loved the odd sisters the moment I first laid eyes on them. So when they found me in my ruined castle, I was tempted to go with them to their home. But I was afraid I would eventually destroy them with my powers. They were so different then, the odd sisters, so different from how they are now. But I don't have to tell you that. You remember how they were. Yes, they'd often speak over each other and become excitable. But now when I look back on my memory of them, I see that they were very different witches from who they are today. Not just because they have aged since then, but because their hearts have changed. Their manners have changed. Their souls have changed. But the sisters then, they wanted to care for me and to take me home with them.

"No matter how they pleaded, I wouldn't go. I was too afraid of what I might do to them.

"'You could never hurt us, dear! No. We will teach you to control your powers.'

"'Oh, yes! We will instruct you, dear!'

"'Please, Maleficent, we love you! We need you!'

"And so it went for quite some time. The odd sisters would come swooping down from the heavens to check on me, and to ask me to live with them. But still I said no.

"Over time, their visits became less and less frequent.

"I kept myself busy with my books and my pets. My crows flew to all the places I was too afraid to travel, told me stories from every kingdom, and brought me spells from other witches. They also brought word from the odd sisters, who kept quite busy with adventures of their own.

"It had been many years since I had seen them when they paid me another visit, again pleading with me to come live with them. It was then that I saw the beginnings of their transformation, although I didn't know it at the time. I only see it now when I look at the events with removed objectivity.

"'You are lonely, dear one,' Lucinda said to me. 'You are withering away with no one to love. Won't you please come to live with us and let us give you the companionship you so desperately need? Please, Maleficent. It is the only way you will survive.'

"That was probably the last visit during which the odd sisters spoke coherently. The next time they visited, everything changed.

"'Maleficent. Please let us help you,' the sisters begged when they came to see me again. 'If you won't come to live with us, if you won't let us love you, then please let us give you a daughter. Let us give you someone to love. Someone to care for and someone who will care for you.'

"I loved the idea of having someone to care for other than my birds. I loved the idea of someone loving me, but I didn't understand how the odd sisters could do this.

"'But how?' I asked. The odd sisters laughed, but not in jest. They laughed because they were happy. They laughed because they thought they were giving me the greatest gift they could give: love. But I was worried. I wasn't sure if this was something I should consider. I wasn't sure if it was safe.

"They assured me it was. 'Oh, my dear, don't fear. We can do this. We've been devising this spell for many years, perfecting and mastering it before we dared to use it.'

"'We would never offer you such a great gift or

dangle it in front of your face if we didn't know we could really give it to you.'

"Lucinda had been doing most of the speaking, but this time it was Ruby who spoke. 'And we would never give you a spell that would put you in danger, dear one. We plan to use the spell ourselves.'

"And then it was sweet Martha, with her slightly kinder eyes, who spoke. 'We created the spell for ourselves, you see, so you know it must be safe. And once it was perfected, once we knew it was finally right and we were about to use it, we had an epiphany!'

"'We should help Maleficent! We will give her this gift!' All the sisters were talking at once, their excitement and love overcoming them. 'We want to give you this, Maleficent! Please let us help you.'

"I couldn't express to them how much their offer meant to me. How wonderful this gift really was, and, yes, of course I would take it. I would have a daughter. I couldn't make myself speak. I couldn't find the words to express my gratitude to them.

"'We know, our dear little dragon fairy-witch,

we know. Please, there is no need for words. Not between us.'

"It was several weeks later when the odd sisters summoned me to their home. They sent a message with Opal, who must have been visiting them on one of her adventures. They said it was finally time to do the spell, but that it needed to be performed at their home. I never left my castle, not ever, not once in all those years, and I was terribly anxious. I was so afraid to use my powers, terrified to use even the simplest of travel charms, that I decided to go by foot to where the odd sisters had placed their house. It was on the outskirts of the kingdom, not very far away at all, but the idea of traveling even such a short distance sent a panic through my entire body. I summoned Diablo, Opal, and my other birds, and I asked them to follow overhead and watch the sky. The odd sisters' letter said that they would have placed their house closer to my castle but something had prevented them from doing so. They assumed it was some sort of security measure by the previous occupant that was remaining in place.

"As I walked through the forest, I felt foolish for being so frightened. But then a desperate need to flee came over me. I sensed that I was in actual danger. The overwhelming feeling of hatred was palpable, and it was then that I knew: it was the forest. It had come to life. It was a terrible thing to behold. The greenery and vines twisted their way toward me with a fearsome velocity. The trees, too, were unlike anything I'd ever seen. They seemed to have faces and long, grasping hands that were impossible to break free from. I thought I was going to die there as the vines wrapped themselves around me while the trees held me fast in place. My birds swooped down, attacking the trees, trying to help me as the thorny vines cut into my flesh and wrapped around my neck. I wasn't frightened as I felt my life force slipping away—not really; it almost felt like a relief. I think I might have been happy to die.

"'Maleficent, no! Use your powers!' the odd sisters screamed through the trees. They stretched their hands toward the sky, turning the world dark with their magic. 'Maleficent! It's dark! Use your magic!'

"In my panic, my body grew warmer and warmer. I'd remembered what you told me in my tree house that afternoon, on the day I first used my travel charm. You said if I ever felt that way again, to just think of somewhere safe, someone I loved, and I'd travel there. That's what I did. Within mere moments, I found myself standing safely on the threshold of the odd sisters' house, no longer in the clutches of my enemy. 'Oh, my goodness, Maleficent! Are you okay?' Lucinda asked.

"I thought I was. I couldn't tell. I think I was in shock.

"'We should have known! We should have known you would be the enemy of nature after what happened in the Fairylands! We were stupid not to have thought of it, we're so sorry!'

"And it made sense even without explanation from the odd sisters. I was the enemy of nature. It seemed only right after I destroyed the Fairylands. I knew I deserved it. It was my curse, and I feared for my daughter. What if I passed my curse on to her?

"'Oh, no! The trees will not condemn her for your deeds! Not to worry!' the odd sisters assured me.

"The inside of the odd sisters' house was very different from my own. It was comfortable, warm, and inviting. It reminded me of my years with you in the Fairylands, with its cozy kitchen and large windows. Outside the large round kitchen window there was even a tree in which my birds could perch. I wondered why I hadn't accepted their offer to bring me there years ago.

"'We're ready to start the spell, Maleficent. But first we need to make you aware of the terms,' Lucinda said.

"Ruby took over. 'The spell only requires the very best parts of you. That way she will truly be your daughter. And in a way, she will be you, but only the very best parts of you.'

"The odd sisters smiled at me. 'We know the spell works, and we promise you, no harm will come to you or your daughter.'

"Lucinda took me by the hand. 'Do you agree to give your daughter the best parts of yourself? Will you let us help you by giving you someone to love?'

"I nodded. 'Yes! I want it more than anything!'

"Lucinda took a crimson drawstring bag filled with a deep bloodred powder from the pocket in her skirt. She poured the powder, which was speckled with ground obsidian crystals, onto the floor in a circle around me. The sisters stood just within the circle, creating a triangle. Lucinda was the pinnacle, while Ruby and Martha flanked me, and their power illuminated their formation with a brilliant silver light. I had absolutely no fear. The odd sisters reflected nothing but love and devotion to me.

"Lucinda began the spell. *We call upon the old gods and the new, to bring a loving daughter to this fairy, to this witch, who is true.* And the three sisters repeated the words over and over again. *We call upon the old gods and the new, to bring a loving daughter to this fairy, to this witch, who is true.*

"I felt a violent jolt to my body and a sensation I couldn't explain—at least, I couldn't then. I can now, because I know now what happened to me. But I will try to describe the sensation as I felt it then. Something was being taken away from me. Honestly, I'm not sure if it was just a strong visceral reaction to the spell, but my body and my soul reacted forcefully. I think it was because I was trying to fight what was happening. Every time the sisters said the words, I was overcome by the same feeling. It was agony.

"*'We call upon the old gods and the new, to bring a loving daughter to this fairy, to this witch, who is true.'*

"The sensation became almost unbearable, and I felt like screaming. I was losing too much of myself. It was as if I was slipping away—becoming nothing. I felt empty and cold. But the sisters had promised they wouldn't hurt me, and I trusted them. Just when I could no longer take the anguish, when I could no longer take the pain and the horrible ripping of my soul, it ended.

"It ended, and I thought perhaps I had died, because surely this was what it felt like to be dead. This was what it felt like to no longer exist. But

I heard the odd sisters' voices in the darkness. I heard them calling to me, calling me back from my pain, calling me back from the nothingness.

"'Maleficent, open your eyes.' It was Martha's voice. 'Maleficent, look, it's your daughter.'

"Lying on the floor at my feet, in the center of the circle, wrapped in a deep purple blanket, was my daughter. She was the most beautiful creature I had ever laid eyes upon, but I had no love for her. I knew I was supposed to love her. I remember wanting to love her before the spell. But I didn't. The only feeling I had was the desire to protect her. But I didn't love my own daughter. I felt empty and alone in a sea of darkness.

"'What will you name her? Do you know?' Lucinda asked as I picked up my daughter for the first time and looked into her beautiful eyes.

"'Her name is Aurora, for she is my shining light in the darkness.'"

CHAPTER XXVIII

Aurora's Nightmare

Aurora felt like she was going mad. The sisters' laughter reverberated through her chamber, causing the images in the mirrors to tremble. It was like being trapped in a small room filled with too many people, all talking at her at once. It was a loud cacophony of voices, punctuated by the odd sisters' hysterical laughter.

In one of the mirrors, she could see her cousin Tulip talking with a giant tree. He was so large that he towered over the highest pinnacle of her castle. In another she saw herself walking down a long passageway, surrounded by an eerie green light. There was something wrong with her eyes.

She looked enchanted, almost like she was asleep. She was being directed toward a spinning wheel. Aurora watched as she touched the spindle and fell to the ground. The sound of a madwoman's laughter filled the air. In yet another mirror, Aurora saw her beloved prince being ambushed by a group of boar-like creatures. The foul beasts were armed with long pointed spears. They had terrible tusks and looked like they came from the very bowels of Hades itself. In a fourth mirror, Aurora saw Maleficent as a young woman, crying. Someone named the Fairy Godmother was telling her it was her destiny to be evil. The younger Maleficent didn't seem evil to Aurora. She appeared smart, loving, and ambitious, but not evil. In another mirror, Aurora saw younger versions of the three good fairies putting a raven in a cage, while in another still, she saw the fairies fighting over the color of a dress they had made for her. Elsewhere, she saw Maleficent speaking to an old woman with silver hair, begging for the woman's help with a spell so that Aurora would never wake.

The images wouldn't stop. They just kept

flashing before her eyes, sometimes too fast for her to understand what was happening. The voices were all speaking at once in a deafening clamor. Aurora saw a young man in a sky-blue velvet jacket with ribbons pacing back and forth in a garden, practicing the words "I love you, Tulip, will you marry me?" over and over. All the scenes were running over each other and creating the most unbearable noise.

"Stop!" Aurora finally yelled. For a moment, everything went still. Then, just as suddenly, the mirrors turned black. The mirrored chamber was eerily quiet. Almost too quiet after all the noise.

"Show me my christening," she said, and watched as the scene appeared in a mirror.

Maleficent was standing in her mother and father's court. She looked hauntingly beautiful in her long black-and-purple robes. Her horns and head were covered in a tight black cowl, creating a menacing effect. This fairy seemed like a completely different person from the teenage Maleficent Aurora had seen in the other mirror. She embodied the spirit of evil.

As the Dark Fairy addressed the court, acknowledging everyone assembled, Aurora could tell Maleficent was angry and hurt. Even though she was stoic and spoke in a pleasant voice, her words were bitter and dripping with despair.

"I really felt quite distressed at not receiving an invitation," she said.

It was made clear to the Dark Fairy that it wasn't a mistake that she hadn't been invited. "You weren't wanted!" Merryweather shouted, trying to charge at the Dark Fairy with her wand drawn. Her friends Flora and Fauna struggled to keep her back.

"Not wanted . . . ahh, oh dear, what an awkward situation. I had hoped it was merely due to some oversight," the Dark Fairy said, stroking her raven Diablo with a sly smile. "Well, in that event, I'd best be on my way."

"And you're not offended, Your Excellency?" asked Queen Leah.

"Why, no, Your Majesty. And to show I bear no ill will, I, too, shall bestow a gift on the child. Listen well, all of you," the terrible fairy commanded as she slammed the end of her staff against the stone floor. "The princess shall indeed grow in grace and beauty, beloved by all who know her. But before the sun sets on her sixteenth birthday, she shall prick her finger on the spindle of a spinning wheel and *die*!"

The odd sisters' laughter echoed through the chamber again. They were laughing so loudly the mirrors in the chamber were threatening to break. "Why do you think the Dark Fairy cared whether or not she was invited to a stupid christening? Why would she have ventured out into the world, something she loathed doing? Something she tried to avoid at all costs? What could possibly compel her to do so?"

Aurora shook her head. "I don't know. It doesn't make sense."

"Our dear sweet girl. It makes all the sense in the world if you know where to look. There are so many invested in your well-being. Even the Dark Fairy holds you in what's left of her heart. She thinks she lost everything the day you were born, but that isn't true. If she didn't still have some part of her old self within her, she wouldn't want to protect you."

"She tried to kill me!" the princess cried.

"She tried to kill you for your own protection! It's degenerative, our dear sweet Rose. Don't you see? We took almost everything that day, but she held on to what was left. She held on to that tiny shining light within her heart," the sisters said with sad smiles as they looked down at the confused princess.

"Please stop talking nonsense!" Aurora shouted. "That doesn't make sense!"

"Oh, it will, my darling. It will. We will explain and show you the truth of your curse, on one condition. First show us our sister!"

CHAPTER XXIX

WITCHES ON TRIAL

Tulip and Popinjay were waiting in the garden. Everything had been arranged to welcome the Fairy Godmother and the three good fairies. Violet brought them a lovely pot of tea accompanied by little finger sandwiches, scones, and tiny tea cakes in pastel colors. Tulip was happy it was a bright clear day. She could see all the way to the cliffs, where the wild, overgrown vines seemed to be lying in wait for Maleficent to come out of the safety of Morningstar Castle. "It's so eerie, isn't it? I wonder why those vines didn't follow her into the castle."

Popinjay thought perhaps he knew. "Oberon, did you have something to do with that?"

Oberon's sonorous laugh echoed in their chests. "You're a clever one, Popinjay. I did indeed!"

"I wonder why Nanny didn't think to do anything about the vines herself. Or Circe," Tulip thought aloud.

"They have many other things to occupy them, little one," Oberon said. "And I am happy to help."

Tulip was just starting to let everything that had happened over the last several days sink in. She hadn't actually had a moment to just sit down and think for what felt like many ages.

"Don't fret, little one. You are handling all of this very well. And you have a good partner in Popinjay here. He may not speak much, but I can see he loves you more than anything in this world," Oberon said, smiling.

Tulip turned a deep shade of scarlet and changed the subject. "There are so many things I don't know about Nanny. It never occurred to me she had such an exciting life before she came to live with me."

Oberon laughed. "Children often don't think of their parents as real people with their own lives.

They see them in a very narrow scope. But your nanny, she is a remarkable fairy and witch. And I know she isn't your real mother, but I imagine she treated you like a cherished daughter."

Tulip nodded. "She did, and still does. I love her very much."

Oberon thought it made sense that Nanny had found herself there. After he had decided to take his slumber, she'd searched every kingdom, trying to find him. He'd loved and appreciated her efforts, but he had lived many lifetimes and he had been tired. It had been time for him to rest. It stood to reason that Nanny would look for Oberon at the place of his origin. And when she had lost her memory, it made sense that she would be drawn to Tulip's family—and to Tulip. "Everything happens for a reason, little one. Nanny might have forgotten who she was for a time, but her heart, her soul, and her reason for living remained. She was drawn to you, just as I was."

Tulip didn't know what to say. "Do you think Nanny is okay?"

Oberon had no fear for Nanny's well-being. "Your nanny is a very powerful witch. Maleficent knows this. And she needs your nanny's help."

Before Tulip could ask Oberon a question that had been plaguing her mind, Hudson arrived in the garden to announce their visitors. He cleared his throat as their guests walked in. "Announcing the ambassador of the Fairylands and former custodian of the princess Cinderella, the Fairy Godmother, who is accompanied by the three good fairies, Merryweather, Fauna, and Flora, the custodians of the princess Aurora."

The fairies looked like they were in very good spirits. "Thank you for receiving us, Princess Tulip," they said in unison.

The Fairy Godmother was dressed in a blue-and-periwinkle hooded cloak, which was decorated with a big pink bow at her throat. Her hair was completely white, not silver like Nanny's. Though Tulip didn't think Nanny resembled the Fairy God-mother, she could see the two were related; they had the same powdery soft skin and grandmotherly quality about them. The three good fairies followed closely behind the eldest fairy. Merryweather was in a long blue gown; Fauna was in green; and Flora was in a red-and-gold gown. All three of them were wearing witches' hats with sashes that kept them securely on their heads. Tulip found that amusing. "Welcome to my court. I'm sorry my mother and father are not here to greet you."

Merryweather looked stricken, and Tulip realized her mistake. "Oh! I'm sorry, I wasn't thinking. I didn't mean . . ."

Fauna flew over to Tulip. "Oh, no, my dear. We just feel simply awful that your parents got caught up in all of this! You have nothing to apologize for. We are the ones who are here to beg your forgiveness."

Tulip was confused. "I thought you were here to discuss the odd sisters." She hadn't intended for her words to come out so matter-of-factly, but they just tumbled out of her mouth. She quickly changed the subject. "Oh, please forgive me, let me introduce you to Prince Popinjay. He is visiting from our neighboring court across the Cyclopean Mountains."

Flora smiled. "Oh, yes, we know all about Prince Popinjay. We've been keeping an eye on you, Tulip, since your . . . ah . . . *encounter* with the Beast Prince."

Tulip flinched at the idea of fairies—albeit good fairies—keeping tabs on her. "I promise you, I am quite well, Flora. I appreciate your concern, but I'm not in need of a good fairy. I have Nanny and Circe for that."

The good fairies' eyes widened. "Circe? We didn't know! Is she here?"

Tulip wondered if the fairies still disliked Circe.

Flora smiled. "We love the work she's done with Belle, and with you, and we are considering asking her if she would like to be an honorary wish-granting fairy."

Tulip was having a hard time connecting these fairies with the fairies from the story Nanny had shared with them. "You're not concerned that she's related to the odd sisters?"

"No, my dear, not one bit. Not since we've sent

them to the realm of dreams," Merryweather said.

Tulip was happy Circe was not there for that conversation. "I'm surprised you would admit your part in the odd sisters' plight so freely, especially here in this house. Circe is a great friend to this family, and she is very distressed at her sisters' state."

Fauna smiled. "Well, dear, we didn't put the odd sisters to sleep *exactly*. We just took advantage of the situation. They were already exhausted by the ordeal with Ursula, and we just thought it would be better if they stayed asleep for a while rather than waking when they regained their powers."

Tulip shook her head. "Better for whom?"

"Well, better for Circe, of course. Better for everyone, really," Merryweather answered.

"Merryweather, I see you are stepping out of your providence again!" Oberon's stern voice bellowed from overhead.

"Oberon?" The Fairy Godmother took flight immediately. "Oberon, it's you! I'm so happy to see you!" She motioned to the three fairies. "Girls, girls! Fly up here at once and meet Oberon!"

The good fairies were beyond excited. "We are so honored to meet you, King Oberon!"

The giant Tree Lord smiled at them. "Yes, yes, little ones, I am happy to meet you, as well! Calm down. Calm down. There are many matters to discuss, many problems for us to solve, but everything should be done in the proper order. First, we have to discuss the matter of the odd sisters. Why have you put them into the realm of dreams? That's not allowed without my permission."

The Fairy Godmother seemed to be thinking it over. "I didn't know you had returned until just now, Great One."

"True, true. You were never as observant as your sister. But you have other talents, which you have displayed remarkably with your charge, Cinderella," Oberon said.

The Fairy Godmother beamed at his praise. "Thank you, Great One."

"But, my dear, my ambassador, I must ask you again why you have taken it upon yourself to banish the odd sisters."

The Fairy Godmother shook her head. "Not banished! Never banished! They are living a beautiful life, my king. They are happier than they have ever been, slumbering in a world of their own design. Tucked away safely where they can no longer hurt anyone."

"Who gave you the right to do that?" Oberon insisted.

The Fairy Godmother thought for a moment. "Why, well, I suppose I did. They have been doing the most terrible things, Great One. They nearly killed Snow White, and drove her mother mad!"

Merryweather chimed in. "Then they almost killed Belle with a foul spell they put on the wolves in the Beast's lands, not to mention how they conspired to kill Ariel and her father, King Triton! And the Fairy Godmother can tell you firsthand the part they played in Cinderella's story!"

"Yes, yes, I know all of this. And something must be done," Oberon agreed. "But my concern is with you, my dearest Fairy Godmother. Why do you feel it's your job to protect all of these girls?

To interfere, even with Tulip here. You've been watching her even though she has been with your sister all this time."

"I didn't know Tulip was her charge. I stopped feeling my sister in the world after she helped me repair the Fairylands. I had no idea it was because she had lost her memory. But once my sister started to remember who she was, I started to feel her in the world once again." The Fairy Godmother stopped for a moment, considering what she was going to say next. "Excuse me, my lord, but when did it become a crime to protect young princesses from harm?"

Oberon thought there was logic in her question. Technically, she was correct. It was a wish-granting fairy's right to look after those in need. And then it became clear to him what bothered him most.

"It's not, my dear. It's not. But let me ask you one thing. Why didn't you find it in your heart to help Maleficent when she was just a tiny little thing, left alone in the crow tree?"

The Fairy Godmother's face dropped. "You've been speaking to my sister."

Oberon laughed his loud, thunderous laugh, though this time it didn't seem he was happy, but instead disappointed. "No, my dear, I saw everything while I slept. I saw all. You left an abandoned child alone to fend for herself. You did everything you could to keep her from flourishing."

The Fairy Godmother's face was stricken with grief. "It's true. Everything you've said is true. And I feel just horrible about it."

The three good fairies joined in. It was like they were singing a cacophonous song of apology. "Oh, we're sorry, too! We really are! We've been trying to do good work in the kingdoms to make up for our part in Maleficent's descent into darkness!"

Oberon considered their words and found truth in them. "I see you are all trying to make up for what happened with Maleficent." He turned to the Fairy Godmother. "And you especially seem to understand it was your words that day that brought about the prophecy."

The Fairy Godmother looked down, ashamed and filled with grief. "I do."

"Then perhaps there is hope for the sleeping princess after all. Perhaps in the admission of your mistakes, Maleficent will see her way to redemption."

The Fairy Godmother shook her head. "Oh, no, not Maleficent. I don't think so. You know she cursed the princess Aurora to prick her finger on a spindle and die! She would be dead now if it weren't for the good fairies' changing the curse to a sleeping curse! And now she intends to kill Prince Phillip to keep him from breaking it!"

Oberon laughed. "Countless stories like this have been told over the years, and how do they end? Always in misery for the wicked queen or witch, always with death. And always she was wronged in some way, by something or some person who set her on this path. It breaks my heart to have to stand against Maleficent, even more so now that you've confirmed it was you who caused this. My only hope is that Maleficent will find a way to redeem herself. My only hope is that she spares the prince and wakes the sleeping princess. But I fear that will not happen."

CHAPTER XXX

Nanny's Failure

Nanny didn't know what to say to Maleficent's story. The two were sitting in silence when Hudson entered the room. He carried a silver tray with a tiny scroll lying on it.

"Excuse me, ma'am, but a message by owl came just now. It's from Circe." He took the tray to Nanny, who picked up the scroll.

"That will be all, thank you, Hudson," Nanny said. As she read the message, she couldn't help letting out a tiny gasp.

"What is it?" asked Maleficent. "Has she found the spell?"

Nanny didn't answer at first.

"What is it?" Maleficent insisted.

"Yes, she's found the spell," Nanny replied.

Maleficent smiled. "Then she is on her way to help us? I knew if she read the spell, she would understand and agree to help me."

Nanny shook her head. "No, she isn't coming."

Maleficent stood, her face green with rage. "Why? Why won't she come?"

"Because, Maleficent, she can't. She isn't here. The odd sisters' house took it upon itself to move locations."

Maleficent remembered speaking to the odd sisters about that long ago, but she thought they were just raving nonsense, as they often did. "Yes. They mentioned there is a fail-safe with the house. I completely forgot! Damn! I should have remembered!" Maleficent started to pace around the room, her robe flowing behind her and her anger growing. "We needed Circe. We needed her powers to break the good fairies' addendum to my curse. We can't do it without her. We need three!"

"Maleficent, calm down! I still don't understand why you cursed your own daughter to die! And to be honest, I don't think anything you say to Circe would persuade her to help you with this! And I don't understand why—"

Nanny stopped herself. She was becoming too familiar with Maleficent, getting too close. She realized that she might be stepping over a boundary if she asked her question.

"What? Why I abandoned my daughter? Why I had the odd sisters give her to you? Don't you see? Do I have to lay it all out for you? Have you not seen what has become of the odd sisters over the years? Do you not detect a change within me? I know you do. I know you can feel it. I can tell you no longer have any love for me. Because I gave Aurora the best parts of myself! The parts of me you loved. I gave them away. There is nothing good left within me. She has all of it, and before my heart became truly corrupt, before I lost myself entirely, I decided to give up my child. I felt myself slipping away by the day. I felt myself becoming cold and empty. I had no love for her, so I wanted you to have her. I wanted you to care for her. I wanted you to have the very best parts of me so that you could have your daughter back, but you gave her away! You gave her to those horrible fairies, even after everything they did to me! You hurt me beyond anything I'd ever experienced. Even when I thought I had lost you, even when I was alone for all those years, that pain was nothing compared to how I felt when you gave my daughter away to those horrible fairies!"

Nanny was heartbroken. "I didn't know! Oh, Maleficent. I'm so sorry. If I'd known the truth, I would never have given her away." Nanny looked at Maleficent with sad eyes, willing herself to have the courage to ask one more question. "Maleficent, I still don't understand why you cursed your daughter to die."

Maleficent's eyes flashed with anger. "Oh, you know. Look into your heart. The answer is there. And if you truly don't know, then it is no fault of mine. You have the power to see time. You could have learned every bit of my story if you chose to! You could have helped me anytime you wished."

Nanny knew Maleficent was right. She could say nothing to defend herself. "You're right, Maleficent. I'm sorry, but we have to save your daughter now.

You can't leave her sleeping in that castle forever. It's not too late to save her and yourself."

"You truly don't know, then. If you did, you wouldn't ask that of me. I can't let my daughter wake. Don't you see—"

But before Maleficent could finish, she heard a choir of screams and gasps. The Fairy Godmother, Flora, Fauna, and Merryweather stood in the doorway, stricken looks on their faces.

"*You're* Aurora's mother?" the Fairy Godmother said.

"We didn't know!" Flora cried.

"Oh, Maleficent, no wonder you hate us!" Fauna gasped.

"I'm so sorry! I'm so sorry we didn't invite you to the christening! Oh, Maleficent! Can you ever forgive us? We didn't know," Merryweather sputtered.

Suddenly, everything made sense. Everything fell into place. But the three good fairies had to protect Aurora—they had to protect their Rose.

They couldn't let her fall into the hands of the Dark Fairy, even if she *was* her mother.

CHAPTER XXXI

THE BOOK OF
FAIRY TALES

Circe and Snow White sat close to each other as the odd sisters' house settled into place. Wherever they had landed, it was dreadfully dark.

"Snow, stay here while I go have a look around," Circe said. "We seem to have stopped."

Snow held on to Circe's hand tightly, not wanting to let go. "I'll come with you."

Together, the two felt their way through the house, stumbling to the largest window. Snow gasped. They were in a sea of darkness surrounded by pools of glittering stars that moved as if they were dancing to music the women could not hear. Bright green and yellow lights streaked across the dark curtain of night—more beautiful than any sunset or sunrise they had ever witnessed.

Circe had no idea where they were, though she had a feeling she knew where they weren't. They weren't anywhere within the many kingdoms. But somehow, inexplicably, she felt safe. "I think the house has moved to its original place. The place of its birth. I remember my sisters talking about this. They warned me it might happen if anything ever happened to them, but honestly, I dismissed it. I regret now how often I didn't listen to their ravings, but everything they said was in fragments and rhymes. It was so hard to understand them."

Snow White was surprisingly composed. "I see. Well, I suppose there's nothing to be done about it. Do you think Nanny received the message you sent?" she asked as she went around the room, lighting the candles on the sconces. Soon the room was filled with light.

Circe blinked, letting her eyes adjust. "I do think she got it. I sent it while we were still in the many kingdoms, before we left the world we know. But I'm afraid there isn't a way to contact her now."

Snow White went to the love seat and picked up the mirror Circe had used to communicate with Nanny. "Can't we use this?"

Circe had forgotten all about the mirror. "Let's try!"

She took the mirror. "Show me Nanny!" Nothing happened. "Show me Maleficent!" Still nothing.

Circe sighed and put down the mirror. Snow seemed to be thinking. "What about the fairy tale book?" she asked. "I wonder if it's still writing everyone's story the way it was when my mother and I looked at it."

"Oh, you are brilliant, Snow. Let's check!" Circe said, opening the book. "It is! Look here! Snow, was this scene here before, between Nanny and Maleficent?"

Snow took the book and read the pages, quickly skimming over the parts of the story she already knew. "This is strange, some of it has changed. Just little bits, here and there. I have no idea how magic works, Circe, but do you think the story is rewriting itself as new events occur?"

Circe wasn't sure, but it seemed like that was a good theory. "It's likely," she said.

"Interesting. I wonder . . ." Snow turned the pages to see what else had changed. "Wait, this story wasn't there before."

Snow saw a beautiful illustration of Circe as a small child. It was unmistakable. In the illustration, Circe was standing with her three older sisters under a brilliant night sky. Snow had never seen so many stars, even in her own enchanted kingdom. She noticed that Circe's sisters were standing around her in a triangular configuration, and there were markings on the ground that glistened in the moonlight. It was an odd illustration, and Snow didn't know what to make of it.

"What? What is it?" Circe asked, seeing the expression on Snow's face.

Snow White wrinkled her nose and pursed her lips. Circe was coming to realize that little habit meant Snow White was concerned. "The story is about you."

Circe felt a jolt of shock move throughout her entire body. "I don't want to see it, Snow! I don't. Please, let's just skip it." Snow gave Circe a look as if to ask if she was sure.

When Circe didn't reply, Snow turned back to the Dragon Witch's story. She skimmed the pages to see if anything else new had been added. As they turned the pages, reading the heartbreaking story Maleficent had shared with Nanny, Circe had to wonder if there wasn't some small part of Maleficent that was still good. Otherwise, Circe figured, she would have already killed the prince. What was holding her back? Circe knew her sisters would have killed him or driven him to some sort of madness by now.

"What is it? What's the matter, Circe?" Snow asked.

The story was so much like Snow's that Circe didn't want to upset her by bringing up dark events from her past.

"I just don't understand why she put the curse on Aurora. Everything else makes sense, I see her motivations. But not that part."

Snow White put her hand on her cousin's cheek and smiled. "That's because you have never had a mother who tried to kill you. As awful as your sisters are, they clearly love you. I know they've lied and they've hurt people. They've hurt you. But after reading what they did for Maleficent, how they tried to help her, it seems to me they were very good witches at one time."

Circe thought that was an extremely kind thing for Snow to say, considering everything her sisters had done to Snow. Then Snow said something that surprised her. "And I think I know why Maleficent cursed her daughter. I think I know why she wanted her to die."

"You do?"

"I think I do. . . ."

CHAPTER XXXII

HER LAST
BETRAYAL

Maleficent could barely contain her rage. Had Nanny arranged this with the fairies, to get her to admit her secrets only to share them with her enemies? She was fuming, on the verge of transforming into her dragon form. *"What is this? How dare you bring them here!"* she cried, her anger threatening to overtake her.

Nanny rushed to her. "Maleficent, no! It's not what you think." But Maleficent raised her staff, creating an invisible force that sent Nanny flying across the room and into the fireplace mantel. "You've betrayed me for the last time!" Maleficent struck her staff on the marble floor. A terrible noise resounded through the castle, and green flames erupted from the fireplace, threatening to engulf Nanny.

"Maleficent! That is enough!"

Maleficent stood stock-still. She didn't know who was speaking or where the voice was coming from.

The Fairy Godmother rushed to her sister and extinguished the flames. She stood in front of Nanny to protect her, her wand ready. "Maleficent, stand back! Don't make me harm you!"

Maleficent laughed at the elder fairy as she searched for the source of the deep, penetrating voice. "Who's there? Who is speaking?" she called out.

She looked around the room, her yellow eyes darting from one place to the next. Nanny hadn't thought Maleficent was capable of fear, but she could tell Maleficent understood the magnitude of Oberon's powers from his voice alone. "Who's there?" she asked again. Maleficent let out a horrible scream as a massive branch smashed through the paned glass and grabbed her.

The three good fairies lifted their wands, creating a silver dome of light to protect everyone from the shards of glass showering down around them. Maleficent was in Oberon's grip. He brought her close to his face so he could see hers. He wanted to see what had become of the fairy. He wanted to see if she was as evil as the other fairies had said. What he saw was more terrible and disappointing than he had imagined. "How dare you hurt your mother! After everything she has done to protect you!"

Maleficent knew who he was. She recognized him from his statue in the fairy courtyard. "Oberon," she said coldly.

The Tree Lord's grip became tighter as he looked deep into the face of the Dark Fairy. "You have no love left within you, foul one. Your heart is filled with hate. You've given me no choice!" He hurled Maleficent through the air toward the threatening forest of vines that had been lying in wait. Oberon's legion of Tree Lords followed her at a startling pace for creatures so large. The earth cracked beneath their heavy footsteps, creating deep canyons and

277

causing the castle and surrounding lands to shake violently and crumble.

As Maleficent flew through the air, she felt herself exploding with heat. She knew what was happening. She was transforming. She let out a horrific scream as a storm of green flames erupted into an inferno that would rival Hades. She circled back to Morningstar Castle, setting everything aflame. Below, Oberon and his Tree Lords hurled giant rocks at her. Maleficent released a torrent of fire on Oberon's army. Her flames exploded onto the ground below, engulfing Oberon's soldiers. With a flap of her wings, Maleficent turned herself toward home.

Diablo! My pet! Gather my birds. Bring them to safety. Bring them home.

Diablo gathered all his mistress's ravens and crows, except for Opal, whom he couldn't find. *Opal! Our mistress needs us.* But she didn't answer. He hoped she hadn't been hurt in the war raging below. But he pushed forward.

Maleficent flew toward her castle as fast as she

could, dodging giant boulders. She knew if she could get to the boundary of her lands, the Tree Lords would not be able to follow. She looked back at the massive army of trees and the terrible forest of vines gaining on her. As she unleashed another stream of flames, she was stuck by a giant boulder. Blood poured from her injured wing, and she felt herself falling toward a large crumbled tower. Maleficent tried to change direction, but her wings were being shredded by the storm of rocks coming at her from all sides, causing her to careen into the tower, destroying it and landing among the rubble. The vines quickly overtook her, wrapping themselves around her. They choked her, binding her mouth closed so she couldn't breathe fire. Maleficent was helpless.

Oberon and his army grew ever nearer. She felt the vibrations of their footsteps in the earth; she felt the unstable ground beneath her starting to give way. They were going to crush her. Maleficent felt their enormous hands reach through the vines again and again, trying to find her in the tangled mess that had engulfed her. She was bleeding as the sharp thorny branches tightly wrapped around her. The vines' thorns pierced her skin, and she was sure she would die there. Then, without even planning it, she found that she was very small once more. In fact, she was so small the trees could not find her in the dense forest of vines. Maleficent was herself again—bleeding and bruised, but herself. She remembered the day she had been attacked on her way to see the odd sisters and how they had turned the sky black to help her.

"I call upon the very furies of hell to bring darkness to these lands and give me the power to overtake these foul abominations of nature!"

The sky became so black that Maleficent couldn't see anything. She was still buried under the vines. "Be still!" she screamed, and the vines froze in the darkness, creating a large opening around the space left by her massive dragon form. Maleficent ran as fast as she could, dodging the Tree Lords' terrible blows as they tried to find her in the tangled forest. Maleficent laughed as she shattered an enormous boulder with her magic before it could crush her. She unleashed her rage, obliterating everything in her path, sending shattering waves of destruction in every direction. Maleficent smashed the vines and splintered some of the Tree Lords into kindling. She even set some of them on fire with a wave of her staff.

Oberon stood in the ruins of the forest, weeping. Holding the smoldering remains of his greatest generals in his arms, he let out a horrible howl that echoed throughout the many lands. His cries caused a downpour of rain that extinguished Maleficent's flames. He had tried to take on the Dark Fairy and lost.

Under cover of darkness, Maleficent made her way safely back to her castle.

Chapter XXXIII

HOME

Maleficent was relieved to be home again. *I have been away for too long*, she mused. She had wasted her time seeking help from those who were destined to betray her. She had been foolish to think she could trust Nanny—to trust anyone other than herself.

The Dark Fairy was alone, just as she had always been. And she would fix her problem herself. She would see to the matter of Prince Phillip.

Maleficent stood in front of the mirror in her dim bedroom. The only light in the room came from the green flames in her fireplace. The light danced, creating menacing shadows of the stone gargoyles peering down at her from the four corners of the room and from either side of the enormous mantel. The gargoyles that flanked the fireplace were taller than her by probably five feet or more. Maleficent had to wonder if they had been living, breathing creatures at one time, because she could on rare occasions detect a tiny glimmer of life within them. Her green face stared back at her in her mirror as she tried to collect herself, reining in her anger. She needed to be clearheaded for this fight. It wasn't just Phillip she was up against. She would be fighting a good portion of the magical realm.

"Maleficent, please stop this now. It's not too late." It was Grimhilde, flickering in her mirror. Maleficent closed her eyes, willing her to go away. She didn't want to see the old queen's face right then. "My friend, I can't let my daughter live. You wouldn't understand."

Grimhilde became quiet and still. "Wouldn't I? I tried to kill my daughter! More than once! If anyone understands, it's me! And mark my words, Maleficent, you *will* die if you face Prince Phillip. It is written in the book of fairy tales. There is no guarantee you will inhabit another realm after your body dies! The odd sisters are not here to protect you!"

Maleficent felt her face burning with anger. "It is all written, then? Predetermined? Why bother to live our lives at all?"

Grimhilde sighed. "I wish there was more I could do, but my powers are limited outside my own kingdom." Grimhilde seemed to understand there was nothing she could say to talk her friend out of this madness. "If you insist on dying today, then please know I have loved you well."

Maleficent felt a lurch in her stomach, in that place where she kept all her pain, in the place where she kept her adoptive mother, the odd sisters, her daughter, and her former self. "I know, Grimhilde. Thank you."

"It's not too late," Grimhilde persisted. "You can release the prince. You can ask the fairies to enchant him so he doesn't remember who you are or what you've done to him. They owe you that much at least! You can wake up your daughter. Just go down to your dungeon and release him, Maleficent. All of this can end!"

Maleficent seemed to be considering everything Grimhilde said. Then her face became rigid. It was hard and almost completely motionless before she said simply, "No."

"Why? Please put aside your pride, and your anger. This isn't about the One of Legends or the other fairies. I know they betrayed you, but please don't let this anger consume you. Don't kill your daughter because others have hurt you. You're not punishing them by doing this. You're hurting yourself! You're hurting Aurora!"

Maleficent wondered why no one saw her motivations in this. It seemed so simple to her, so obvious. But no one, not even those who had once been closest to her, knew her reason. The odd sisters would understand, though they would've wanted to keep the princess awake, and they'd have reveled in the disaster they created by doing so.

"I have to kill Phillip. Don't you see? He is her true love. They fell in love with each other without even knowing they were betrothed. He has renounced his place in his father's kingdom for his love of her, without knowing that it is she he is intended to marry. If he kisses her, she *will* wake up! It's all too perfect, really. Predestined, like it was written many years ago and the two are just playing their parts. And of course, I've played my part, the mistress of all evil, determined to keep the young lovers apart! And why? Because I was offended by being left off a guest list? No! Was it my adoptive mother's betraying me and giving my daughter to those horrible fairies that caused me to want to see my daughter die on her sixteenth birthday? It all seems so simple, doesn't it? There are so many mundane reasons to choose from. But no one sees the truth. No one sees why I need to keep my daughter safe!"

She threw her staff across the room in anger, making a loud clatter. "Why do you think I chose her sixteenth birthday? Do you think I just picked an arbitrary number out of the ether? I came into my powers on my sixteenth birthday and I destroyed the Fairylands. I almost killed everyone I loved when I came into my powers, and I don't want that for my daughter. She will have my powers. She's probably already showing signs of them now! I don't want her to suffer the way I have. I'm trying to save her that pain. She needs to stay in the land of dreams!"

Grimhilde understood. She understood more than anyone else ever could. "I understand. And I agree."

"You do? Truly?"

"I do. If you think she has your powers, if there is any chance, any chance at all, you have to protect her. You mustn't let her wake, even if you have to kill Prince Phillip."

"Thank you, my friend."

"Now go, save your daughter!"

CHAPTER XXXIV

MISTRESS OF
ALL EVIL

Maleficent was in the bowels of her castle, where she did her great magic. *My important magic.* Her goons were there, dancing in the green flames, as she stroked her beloved Diablo. She had to cast everyone and everything out of her mind. She had made herself vulnerable in the past few days and had been betrayed. She was alone, and she belonged to the crows. The creatures danced in her honor. They belonged to her, and they did her bidding. She started to feel like her old self, the way she had felt before she ventured to Morningstar Kingdom. Her power was returning to her in this place, her home, her place of strength. She knew she was the Dark

Fairy, but she wondered: Did she really have to kill him? Did she have to kill the prince?

As her goons danced in the flames, she thought of Phillip, alone in his cell, and her hatred for him grew. He was a threat to her daughter's security. And she would do anything to keep her daughter safe. To keep her from becoming the monster she herself was. And as she stroked her pet Diablo while they watched the festivities, she thought she'd better pay the prince a visit. "What a pity Prince Phillip can't be here to enjoy the celebration. Come, we must go to the dungeon and cheer him up."

Diablo led the way down the long hall that was guarded by his mistress's goons. They went down a long, narrow cylindrical staircase that wrapped around the east end tower, even farther into the depths of the castle. It led to the dungeon, where Maleficent had told her minions to imprison the prince. Diablo perched on a protruding column while his mistress used a skeleton key to unlock the large wooden door, which groaned in a warning when she opened it. She found Prince Phillip much the way she expected to, chained to the wall with his head down. He was exhausted and in despair. Was she really doing this? Was she going to kill him? Was she taking on the role of the Dark Fairy? The mistress of all evil? But she'd already resigned herself to the role. *This is the way it was written. This is how it was meant to be.*

"Oh, come now, Prince Phillip, why so melancholy? A wondrous future lies before you. You, the destined hero of a charming fairy tale come true." The mistress of all evil waved her hand over the sphere at the top of her staff, enchanting it so the prince could see into his future. Maleficent decided that she didn't have to play the role exactly. She could take another path. Maybe she could save the prince and still keep her daughter safe. And maybe, just maybe, Maleficent would live. "Behold, King Stefan's castle. And in yonder topmost tower, dreaming of her true love, the princess Aurora. But see the gracious whim of fate: why, 'tis the selfsame peasant maid who won the heart of our noble prince but yesterday. She is indeed most wondrous fair;

gold of sunshine in her hair; lips that shame the red, red rose; in ageless sleep she finds repose. The years roll by, but a hundred years to a steadfast heart are but a day, and now the gates of the dungeon part, and our prince is free to go his way. Off he rides on his noble steed, a valiant figure straight and tall, to wake his love with Love's First Kiss and prove that true love conquers all." Maleficent laughed at the evil brilliance of her plan. She laughed as she saw the prince struggling against his chains, realizing she intended to keep him there for a hundred years. "Come, my pet, let us leave our noble prince with these happy thoughts. A most gratifying day."

As she locked the dungeon door behind her, she felt relief wash over her. "For the first time in sixteen years, I shall sleep well." Maleficent made her way to her tower, comforted by the thought that her daughter was safe. She wanted to sit and think. She wanted to talk over her plan with Grimhilde to see if she thought Maleficent had made the right decision in keeping the prince alive, but Diablo was making a terrible screeching noise. She heard the clamor of weapons and thought her goons were fighting among themselves, being the witless fools that they were.

"Silence! You tell those fools to—Ah! No!"

My precious one. My old friend.

Diablo had been turned into stone! And she knew who was responsible.

The three good fairies!

CHAPTER XXXV

THE DARK
FAIRY'S DEMISE

Aurora didn't understand why the odd sisters didn't simply say their little sister's name to make her appear in the mirror. They stood baleful and wraithlike before her in their tattered white dresses. *Wait. When did they change their dresses?* Aurora's head was spinning. *Is any of this real? Why are these witches tormenting me?*

"Because, my dear, this is your dream. We have invaded your corner of the dreamscape, and you control the mirrors here. Now say our sister's name! Show us Circe!"

Reluctantly, Aurora did as they asked. "Show me Circe."

Images of Circe appeared in all the mirrors, but the one in the mirror on the right-hand side of the chamber caught Aurora's eye. That Circe seemed to be staring directly at Aurora. It sent chills down Aurora's spine that she couldn't explain. There was something unnerving about that image of Circe. It was as if she could see right into the princess's very soul. But the sisters didn't seem to notice; they were focused on another mirror, where Queen Grimhilde was screaming at Circe, threatening to kill her. "I will see the queen Grimhilde rot in the bowels of Hades for this!" Ruby screamed, but Lucinda was now concerned with what was happening in one of the other mirrors. "Shhh! Sisters, I don't think that's happened yet! But look!"

In the other mirror, Circe was at home, searching through the odd sisters' books, desperately looking for something. "Oh, Snow! I think I found it. I think I found what Maleficent was talking about. It's a spell!" Circe said, panicked. The odd sisters watched as all the color ran from Circe's face. She looked ill, like she might faint.

"What is it?" Snow asked, running to Circe and putting her tiny hand in hers. "Are you okay? Come sit down over here. I will get you some more water. You look dreadful."

"Take your hands off our sister!" Ruby shouted. But Snow White couldn't hear her.

"What is that horrible brat queen doing in our house?" Martha yelled, but Lucinda quieted her sisters. She wanted to hear what Circe was saying.

"I understand now. It all makes sense. Everything. Every foul deed. My sisters' mania. My powers. Everything."

"No!" The odd sisters' screams filled the chamber, but they were distracted by some of the mirrors that were now flashing images of Maleficent.

"Sisters, look! It's Maleficent!"

Ruby shot Aurora a wicked look. "Why are you changing the mirrors? We asked to see our sister!"

"Ruby! Look! The Tree Lords are going to kill Maleficent!" Martha cried.

"This isn't how she dies! This isn't how it ends!" Lucinda screamed, panic-stricken.

"No, Sisters, look!" Ruby said, pointing at another mirror, where the prince was escaping Maleficent's castle on his white horse with the help of those wretched good fairies. From the parapet of her castle, Maleficent waved her glowing staff, summoning her dark magic. Shouting the words of her evil spell, Maleficent took control of the thorny vines, making them encircle King Stefan's castle.

"Good girl!" Lucinda yelled. "You control the darkness, evil one! Make a dark storm! Surround the castle with thorns!" She looked to her sisters. "This is what's happening now! She is pursuing the prince!"

Lucinda was worried about the good fairies' helping the prince, and she was fearful they would overcome Maleficent. She took a little crescent moon-shaped sickle from her bodice belt and sliced her hand. She held her hand open, palm up, and let the blood pool there until there was so much it started to seep between her fingers, dripping onto the floor. "Sisters, come."

Ruby and Martha held out their long, clawlike

hands, letting Lucinda slice open their palms with a quick unceremonious gesture. Aurora watched in horror as the odd sisters placed their bloodstained hands on the mirror while Lucinda said the words: "Let us help this witch, this fairy true, and see into her heart and give her her due."

The odd sisters started to convulse, shaking uncontrollably as they repeated the words, this time more loudly than before.

"Let us help this witch, this fairy true, and see into her heart and give her her due."

The odd sisters could now see into the Dark Fairy's heart. They knew she wanted to kill the prince. They could feel what she felt—all her sorrow, her loneliness, her anger and pain. The weight of it was crushing.

This is how the story goes. This is who I am and who I was always destined to be. I am the mistress of all evil.

The odd sisters felt cold hearing Maleficent say those words. In a confusing flash, they saw the young Maleficent, they saw themselves young, all of them different, much different from how they were now. They remembered the young girl they had loved, the young girl they had hoped would never see this day. The little witch fairy they wanted to protect. Suddenly, without understanding why, their perspective changed; they were brought back into themselves, feeling quite different, quite like themselves again. They were eager to see Maleficent embrace her powers and her dark destiny. To see her control the darkness and use it to her advantage. They'd always known this day might come, even if there had been a time when they wished it wouldn't. The witches they were now knew that it was meant to be, and that they themselves had played an even larger role than the Fairy Godmother in bringing Maleficent here, to this place in time. The time Nanny had always seen. The time Nanny had dreaded with all her being.

Nanny just hadn't seen them, the odd sisters. Hiding behind the mirrors. Where they always were.

The odd sisters knew Maleficent wouldn't betray herself. They knew she was no longer afraid to kill the prince, especially now that he was thrashing his way through the forest to the sleeping Aurora. She was the mistress of all evil! But they were brought out of their reverie by Aurora's terrible screams as Maleficent stood confidently against the prince, a green inferno surrounding her. The foes faced each other on the drawbridge of King Stefan's castle, Maleficent's powers reaching their apex. The sisters had never seen her so powerful. Aurora's hysterical crying was distracting them. Lucinda put her hand on Aurora's face, almost tenderly at first, and then pushed her backward. The princess fell gently, almost as if she were floating in reverse onto the floor.

"Sleep, child! Sleep in the land of dreams!" the sisters cried together.

Martha gasped as she saw Maleficent erupt into a tempest of black and purple storm clouds, growing and towering over the castle. They were connected to her, by spell craft and by blood. The sisters began to tremble violently again, their hands bleeding all over their tattered white dresses and staining their porcelain skin. The first to fall to the floor was Ruby, then Martha. Lucinda stood over them, doing what she could to comfort her sisters and keep them from injuring themselves while they convulsed. They were sprawled on the floor, shaking and screaming unintelligibly, their eyes rolled back into their heads. Then, suddenly, they went completely quiet and still. Their eyes bulged from their deep-set sockets. Lucinda could see only the whites of their eyes, and she knew she could now communicate with Maleficent through her sisters. She put her right hand on Ruby's heart and her left on Martha's, making a deep red bloodstain on her dress from the cut her in hand.

"Embrace your destiny, Maleficent! Die if you must to keep your daughter safe!" Lucinda screamed. She smiled as she heard Maleficent say the words.

"Now shall you deal with me, oh Prince! And all the powers of hell!"

Lucinda watched as Maleficent grew, towering above the storm clouds that were crashing and erupting in the tumultuous sky. She could feel the power surging through Maleficent as she transformed, making her feel more wondrous than ever before, and Lucinda knew in her heart that Maleficent was finally herself.

Her true self.

The mistress of all evil.

As Maleficent transformed into a magnificent beast, she didn't feel pain. How she loved being in this dragon form. She wished she had embraced her evil long before; perhaps then her transformations wouldn't have been so painful. If only she hadn't resisted who she really was for so long. She reveled in destroying the prince. She wanted to taste his blood and feel his bones snap within her powerful jaws. *I'm going to save my daughter. Time to die!* Her terrible jaws snapped at Prince Phillip, the pain from the blows of his sword not even registering. She had one purpose. She would kill the prince to save her daughter. And she would enjoy it. She would stand watch for an eternity, protecting Aurora from anyone who dared try to wake her. Nothing else mattered. Everything had been building to that moment. She was free. She would finally be able to give her daughter the one thing no one had ever been able to give Maleficent: peace.

Lucinda's scream echoed in Maleficent's ears. "The sword! They're enchanting the sword!" But it was too late.

"Now Sword of Truth, fly swift and sure, that evil die and good endure," Flora chanted.

The prince threw the enchanted sword into the dragon's heart. Her scream echoed through the many kingdoms, reverberating in the hearts of those who had once loved the Dark Fairy. They felt her pain as she used her last breath to blast the prince with fire before she fell over the precipice to her demise. The prince expected to find the dragon's body lying at the base of the cliff, but he saw only his sword plunged into Maleficent's empty tattered robes. It was over. The young prince had taken Maleficent's life so he could begin his own.

CHAPTER XXXVI

CIRCE'S WRATH

Lucinda knew there was nothing she could do to save Maleficent. It was over. No spell would bring her back to life, and there was no body to resurrect. There was nothing left of the Dark Fairy. She looked at her sisters on the floor and decided not to wake them. She was too exhausted to deal with the inevitable theatrics bound to overtake the dreamlands when her sisters learned that the Dark Fairy had lost her battle with Prince Phillip. The only thing that gave Lucinda comfort was the knowledge that Maleficent was finally free of torment—that in her last moments she felt happy, because she had embraced who she really was.

"No!" Circe screamed from one of the mirrors.

Lucinda spun around frantically, searching for her daughter.

"I'm right here," Circe snapped, glaring at Lucinda from the rightmost mirror.

Lucinda had never seen Circe so angry, and so sad. "My darling! I'm happy to see you," Lucinda said.

"Maleficent's death is on your hands! That foul spell wouldn't have worked if she hadn't embraced evil! You've meddled in the lives of too many people. You've caused too much death. Too much destruction!"

"We only wanted to help her, Circe! We gave her someone to love!"

"And you destroyed her in the process. You took everything away from her and gave it to that girl lying on the floor! Maleficent didn't start to become evil until you performed that spell to create Aurora, just as you destroyed yourselves by creating me!"

Lucinda shook her head. "Circe, no! You don't understand!"

"I understand everything, Mother. And if you ever want to walk in the waking world again and see me in the flesh once more, you will wipe that girl's memory clean. You will make sure Aurora has no memory of these events. None whatsoever! And you will stop tormenting Snow White in her dreams! Do you understand?"

"I do," Lucinda said soberly, taking her daughter very seriously.

"Now, do you think Aurora has inherited her mother's powers?" Circe asked.

Lucinda thought about Maleficent's greatest attributes. Her power was one of them. "Well, my darling daughter. You inherited *our* powers. I have to assume Aurora inherited her mother's, as well."

"I see." Circe seemed to be thinking, wondering what to do.

Lucinda sighed. "This isn't how this story was supposed to end."

"It's exactly how it was meant to end. It's the only way it *could* have ended from the moment you and your sisters came crashing into Maleficent's life! You destroy everything you touch! You're vile torrents of destruction, ruining everything in your wake!"

Lucinda was speechless. She just stood there, letting her daughter's words flow over her like a deluge of grief. "Will we ever see you again?"

Circe looked at her mother. "If you do what I've asked of you, I will consider it. If you don't, then no, you will never see me again!"

"I will do what you've asked. But you have to do the spell that binds Aurora's powers. I'm not strong enough, not from here. Do it soon. The prince is on his way to the castle. He's about to wake the sleeping princess with his kiss. Look in the book of fairy tales and see the mirror you're meant to use to complete the spell. You will find the mirror in my room."

Circe wanted to ask her mother many questions. She wanted to know how her mother knew that part of the story would be in the book of fairy tales. She wanted to know if the dreaded three had spellbound the book. She wanted to know what had happened to Ruby and Martha. But there wasn't time. She needed to bind the princess's powers.

Circe would do this last thing for Maleficent. She would make sure Maleficent hadn't died in vain.

Lucinda motioned for her to leave. "Go, Daughter, now! I will take care of things here. You go and do your magic."

Chapter XXXVII

Twice Upon a Time

Circe stood in her mothers' house. She was exhausted and numb, staring at the empty mirror that no longer held her mother's reflection.

"Circe! What happened?" Snow White asked. She looked frightened, and Circe couldn't blame her. Everything had been thrown into chaos when Aurora had called Circe to the mirror. Even now, she didn't understand how the princess had managed it. "I need to see the book of fairy tales, quick!"

Snow grabbed the book and handed it to Circe. Circe flipped through the pages to find what she was seeking. "Look here, Snow! She was right! I bind Aurora's powers using this mirror!"

And before she ran into her mothers' room to perform the spell, she hugged Snow tightly, not wanting to let go. Circe was so happy to have Snow White there with her. She didn't know what the following days would bring or how they would find their way out of that dark place. She didn't know what would become of her mothers or whether she would decide to wake them. But she did know, for the first time, that she had a true family in Snow White, Nanny, and Tulip, and she wanted nothing more than to get back to Morningstar Castle so she could tell Nanny and Tulip the rest of Maleficent's story.

THE END